A MYSTERIOUS JOB CALLED ODA NOBUNAGA
1

Kisetsu Morita
◆ Illustration by Kaito Shibano ◆

YEN ON
NEW YORK

A Mysterious Job Called
Oda Nobunaga, Vol. 1
Kisetsu Morita

Translation by Alex Wetnight
Cover art by Kaito Shibano

ODA NOBUNAGA TOIU NAZONO SHOKUGYO GA MAHO KENSHI YORI CHEAT DATTANODE, OUKOKU WO TSUKURU KOTONI SHIMASHITA volume 1
Copyright © 2017 Kisetsu Morita
Illustrations copyright © 2017 Kaito Shibano
All rights reserved.
Original Japanese edition published in 2017 by SB Creative Corp.

This English edition is published by arrangement with SB Creative Corp., Tokyo in care of Tuttle-Mori Agency, Inc., Tokyo.

English translation © 2020 by Yen Press, LLC

Yen On
150 West 30th Street, 19th Floor
New York, NY 10001

Visit us at yenpress.com
facebook.com/yenpress
twitter.com/yenpress
yenpress.tumblr.com
instagram.com/yenpress

First Yen On Edition: May 2020

Yen On is an imprint of Yen Press, LLC.
The Yen On name and logo are trademarks of Yen Press, LLC.

The publisher is not responsible for websites (or their content) that are not owned by the publisher.

Library of Congress Control Number: 2019942581

ISBNs: 978-1-9753-0556-7 (paperback)
       978-1-9753-0557-4 (ebook)

10 9 8 7 6 5 4 3 2 1

LSC-C

Printed in the United States of America

© Kaito Shibano

"My job is
Akechi
Mitsuhide..."

—Alsrod,
this woman may
you.

A MYSTERIOUS JOB CALLED ODA NOBUNAGA

1

Map of the Kingdom of Therwil

Fort Saura

Holai Castle

Mineria Castle

FORDONERIA
PREFECTURE

BRANTAAR
PREFECTURE

Maust Castle

Nayvil Castle

Fort Nagraad

Fordoneria Cathedral

OLBIA
PREFECTURE

© Kaito Shibano

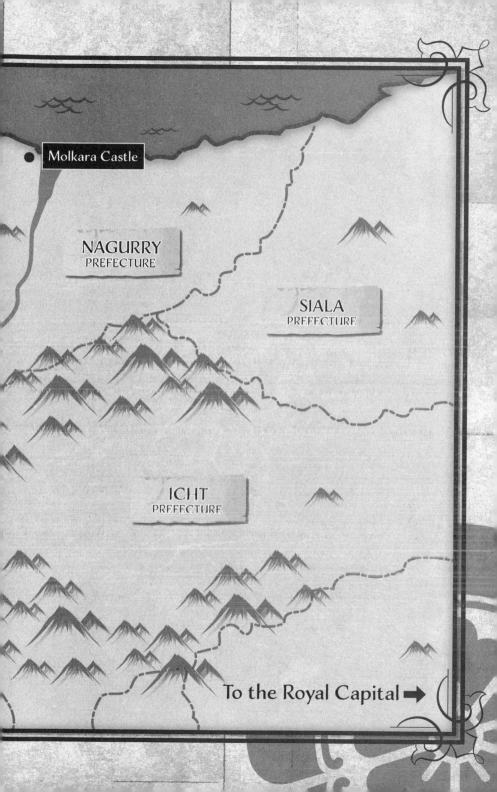

Oda Nobunaga

Mysterious entity and Alsrod's "profession," who often speaks to Alsrod. Is really Oda Nobunaga, a conqueror from another world.

Alsrod Nayvil

Second son of the Nayvil domain's previous lord. Received a mysterious job called Oda Nobunaga during his profession-bestowal ceremony at age eighteen, instantly altering his destiny from that day forward...

A MYSTERIOUS JOB CALLED ODA NOBUNAGA

❖ ⟡ ❖

CHARACTER PROFILES

❖ ⟡ ❖

Illustration by Kaito Shibano

Seraphina Caltis

Daughter of Ayles Caltis. Has the highly rare profession of Saint.

Laviala Aweyu

Alsrod's milk sister and half-elven childhood friend. A well-rounded, good natured young lady skilled in combat and strategy.

Geisel Nayvil

Lord of the Nayvil domain. Oppresses his younger half brother, Alsrod, who was born to a concubine.

Altia Nayvil

Alsrod's sickly younger sister. Worries about her lowly ranked brother's safety.

Ayles Caltis

Ruthless leader of Brantaar Prefecture. In conflict with the neighboring Nayvil clan.

Kivik Klute

A veteran commander serving the Nayvil clan. Defends Fort Nagraad on the border with Brantaar Prefecture.

Kelara Hilara

A military officer serving Hasse. Skilled with both the pen and the sword. Clever and knows her history. Profession: Akechi Mitsuhide.

Hasse

Cousin of the current king and son of the last. A wanderer who seeks to retake the throne.

A MYSTERIOUS JOB CALLED ODA NOBUNAGA

CONTENTS

1   A Job Called Oda Nobunaga · · · · 001

2   A Life-or-Death Siege · · · · · · · · · · · · · 009

3   One Night at the Fort · · · · · · · · · · · · 023

4   Promoted to Baron for My
    Military Achievements · · · · · · · · · · · 033

5   Usurping the Viscount · · · · · · · · · · · 043

6   The Largest Territory
    in Clan History · · · · · · · · · · · · · · · · · 053

7   From Viscount to Count · · · · · · · · · 071

8   Becoming Count of Fordneria · · 091

9   Castle Relocation and an Heir · 111

10   My Sister's Marriage and
    the New Castle · · · · · · · · · · · · · · · · · 129

11   Unification and a Noble Lady
    as Concubine · · · · · · · · · · · · · · · · · · 141

12   The Invasion of Nagurry · · · · · · · · 159

13   Instating the Crown Prince · · · · · · 173

BONUS   Alsrod's Birthday Party · · · · · · · · · · 193

I was born into the ruling class, but I never once felt fortunate. That was because I was the ruler's second son. My older brother—already ten years old—was the heir, and what's more, I was the child of a concubine. When I was three, my mother died from complications after giving birth to my little sister, and my father died of illness when I was ten.

Because of that, for the past several years, I had lived thoroughly in the shadow of my half brother. He was the legitimate ruler of the domain, and I was treated as one of his vassals. I was granted only half of a small village; on top of that, I was forced to fight in wars with neighboring domains even though I was not yet a full-fledged adult.

But my days of misfortune were about to end.

"You're in an awfully good mood, Lord Alsrod," my attendant, Laviala, remarked as she helped me get dressed. Formal wear couldn't be put on by oneself alone because of the buttons on the back.

"I guess it's easy to tell, huh?"

"Of course. I've been by your side for seventeen years!"

Laviala was one of my few vassals, though she was really like a child-hood friend. A descendant of elves, she consequently had pointed ears and beautiful golden hair. As the daughter of my wet nurse, who suck-led and raised me, Laviala was also my milk sister. Plus, she and I were the same age, making her basically like family.

If anything, the fact that Laviala was my milk sister at all was hard proof of my low social status. Elves were not regarded very highly in this land; I was therefore given to an elvish nurse to cement the superiority of my brother, our father's legitimate son. Needless to say, I'd never distance myself from Laviala over such a thing, though.

"Today, I'll join the world of adults. It's finally time for my profession-bestowal ceremony." In this country, when a person came of age, they went to the temple and learned their calling in what was called a profession-bestowal ceremony. By listening to the voices of the gods, the priest could discern what job that person was best suited to.

Of course, that didn't mean they'd be able to support themselves their whole life in that profession. In most cases, all it meant was that they were a bit better at it than the average person. In other words, if a farmer's son was told, "Your profession is Fighter," it just meant he was somewhat physically strong; he was almost certainly not going to be able to become a soldier and make a living off it.

Now, it was said that your abilities improved depending on your profession, so the Fighter job might be of use if the man was called to war, but that was about it. A ruler couldn't possibly quit being a ruler just because he was told Fighter suited him better, so he'd probably just try to have an active role in battle. For that reason, the profession bestowed at one's ceremony was often referred to as the "apposite profession," separate from one's actual occupation. However, in rare instances, you might be given an extraordinarily powerful profession that would end up altering your life profoundly.

One example was Spellsword, a profession for heroes exceptionally skilled in both magic and swordsmanship. It was said that all those who'd established dynasties in the past had been Spellswords. If I could join their ranks and make my mark, even my asshole brother would have to recognize my talent. The central royal family, as troubled as they were, might come to demand my direct services as my fame grew. I could finally be something more than just the second son of a minor lord, with virtually no rights and doomed to risk my life in endless wars!

There were also professions like Sage or Monk, which might give me the opportunity to leave here and go to the capital city for study. And a skilled Sage or Monk could serve using magic, so there was a good chance my brother would let me go.

So how could I not be excited?

"I'm gonna be a Spellsword, no matter what."

To that end, I'd devoted myself to reading books on magic and working on my swordplay. Everything I did was part of my effort to close in on becoming a Spellsword. I figured if the gods could recognize our predispositions, surely someone's profession would be something they were already good at. The possibility was strong, at least.

"Personally, I'd like to see you become a Sage and join a research institute, since the Kingdom of Therwil is in the middle of the Hundred Years' Rebellion," said Laviala. "...All right, you're all done getting dressed!" She smiled cheerfully as she came back around to face me.

"It'd be great if we could avoid fighting, but we'd otherwise get wiped out by the surrounding lords." The royal family of Therwil, a kingdom with a three-hundred-year long history, had seen its power weaken, prompting the various lords of the realm to begin seizing land from one another and falling into a state of civil war—commonly known as the Hundred Years' Rebellion. It was also the reason why our people had to leave for battle all the time.

"Whether we fight or we hope for peace, we can't go wrong by being powerful."

"Yes, I am well aware of your sagacity, my lord... I pray there is glory waiting in your future," Laviala replied, joining her hands as I gently stroked her head.

"Thanks. I want to become the sort of man who can share his glory with you, if at all possible."

And so I made my way with Laviala toward a temple in the domain.

"Ah, the viscount's brother, Lord Alsrod. This way, please."

Since it was a lord's job to financially support the temples in his domain, the priests treated me pretty well. The old priest took me in front of one deity's statue.

© Kaito Shibano

"I will begin the profession-bestowal ceremony. Please lower your head. Now I shall convey which profession the gods have decided is for you. Until I say you may open your eyes, please close them and remain still."

"Right. Go ahead."

I felt Laviala watching over me from afar.

Please say Spellsword! Please, please, please! My whole life depends on this!

I guess the priest must've been listening to the voices of the gods—what followed was a long, long silence. Time stands still when no one's talking......

....

....

Although, um, isn't this unusually long?

"O gods... Wh-what could this be...?" the priest murmured to himself. Odd.

Perhaps they'd opted for a particularly outrageous profession? In extremely rare instances, you could receive a sort of upgraded version of a profession, such as Grand Wizard or Great Sage. If that happened, your skill potential would be much greater, and naturally the likelihood of finding success would be, too. It wasn't such a bad thing.

"So it is no mistake... Please forgive me, O gods, for doubting your divine will..." The priest was in total shock.

Here we go—my future begins now!

"Please open your eyes."

I did as I was told and turned toward the priest. "So what's my profession?"

"Your profession...is Oda Nobunaga."

"Oda Nobunaga?"

I'd certainly never heard of that before. I didn't even have a clue what sort of work it would entail. "I'm sorry, but this 'Oda Nobunaga,' as you say—what sort of job is it?"

"The gods did not explain any further... However, they were very clear that it is Oda Nobunaga—"

"That's absurd! How am I supposed to know how to pursue this profession if I don't even know what it is?!" I was dumbfounded. I'd waited for this day for so long... All that effort put into becoming a Spellsword, only to be told "Oda Nobunaga"... "This is some kind of mistake! Please, ask the gods again!"

"I cannot question what the gods have decreed—though I, too, was uncertain and had to confirm with them that this unheard-of profession is indeed correct. They indicated it is. The decision cannot be changed."

You must be joking... Do I have to live my life from here on out with this "Oda Nobunaga" profession? What language is that? Is it a word from some regional dialect?

"In—in any case... Lord Alsrod, you have been graced with the profession Oda Nobunaga. If you live in accord with this blessing, doubtless you will have the promise of peace and success."

What a load of bullshit... Just what does "living in accord with Oda Nobunaga" even mean?

"I could be mistaken, but you weren't asked by my brother to spite me or anything like that, were you?" My brother was the lord of the domain; not even a priest could disobey him. Without the lord's support, all the money required for religious rites and more would be gone. It wasn't uncommon for temples to fully collude with their lords; sometimes the priest would actually be a member of their lord's family.

"Goodness, no! I simply passed on the words of the gods as they were spoken." He clearly wasn't lying. That didn't change my situation, however...

My dejection must have been written on my face, because when I returned to Laviala, the first words out of her mouth were "Oh no. Cheer up?"

"I certainly won't. I doubt I'll even get out of bed for the next few days."

"Did you get some sort of awful profession? Something of no use even in battle, like Singer or Baker?"

"At least then I'd know what I should be doing. My suitable profession was Oda Nobunaga…"

I expected Laviala to simply be at a loss for words, but instead, she pulled me into a tight embrace.

"L–Laviala…?"

"Does this make you feel better…? I mean, they say humans feel at ease when hugged…" She was obviously very worried about me. "It must have been so hard for you…having worked so much for this day, only for this…"

"Thanks, Laviala. I already feel better. Looks like I won't need to stay in bed after all." Grieving wouldn't change anything for the better—I should at least stay positive. "Now I know what my job is, and that makes me an adult. I can't just sit here and sulk like some little kid. I'll lighten up."

"That's wonderful, Lord Alsrod!"

"Besides, Oda Nobunaga could always turn out to be some sort of incredibly powerful job."

All I could do was hope for a miracle.

When I reported to my brother at Nayvil Castle, he couldn't contain his laughter.

"Ha-ha-ha! To think you'd get such a bizarre job! And here you put so much effort into becoming a Spellsword... Such a shame, really!"

He infuriated me, and I hated that I couldn't just say *Actually, Oda Nobunaga is a really awesome job* or anything like that.

"I received Fighter as my profession. I thought that was ho-hum, but at least it's better than *Oda Nobunaga*. I should be thankful to the gods." His lackeys were snickering.

No need to act so high and mighty. The Nayvil domain, ruled by the Nayvil clan, was just a small power, after all.

A domain was vaguely defined concept—it wasn't the same as a prefecture or the counties within, or the towns and villages within that. For example, the Nayvil domain consisted of the land controlled by the Nayvil clan, centered around Nayvil County. Because the Nayvil clan's land stretched beyond that of Nayvil County, Nayvil County and the Nayvil domain didn't match up exactly.

If we were to enter a full-fledged war with Mineria to the west, we'd be in danger of getting wiped off the map. More precisely, we had no room for error whatsoever. That was another reason why I'd never been happy to be part of the ruling class. Maybe this wasn't as true for a powerful lord, but it wasn't uncommon for weaker lords to be killed for even a single political misjudgment. Sometimes I thought I'd almost rather be a peasant, unconcerned with such fears.

"Come to think of it, the first time you went out to battle as a Fighter, didn't you suffer a devastating loss?"

My brother's face turned red. So predictable. He'd never been good at combat. In fact, despite the fact that he was a Fighter, I was sure he'd never actually taken down an enemy on his own.

"M-mind your own business!"

Speak for yourself.

A few of his vassals who'd served during our father's reign grimaced at my brother's immaturity. They must have realized how incompetent he was.

Professions provided better bonuses the stronger you got. For Fighter, it was said that both attack and defense saw an automatic 20 percent improvement. Such stories were believable enough. You often heard about people becoming unrecognizable after their profession-bestowal ceremonies because of how much stronger they became. So it was practically unheard of that a Fighter would lose one-on-one to someone without a combat profession—but that just went to show how much Geisel must have neglected his sword practice.

"Regardless, Alsrod, you are now undoubtedly an adult. That itself is worth celebrating."

"Thank you very much, Brother." Finally, a semblance of fraternalism.

But then he once again laughed contemptuously. "So listen. Those Minerian bastards are attacking one of our castles, and I want to deploy you right away as general. It's a small fort, but it's an important point of defense for our domain. Defend it with your life."

"Is that Fort Nagraad?" That was the front line. One mistake would mean death.

"Indeed. As their lord's younger brother, your arrival would raise the troops' morale. Drive out the Minerians. If you flee or allow the fort to get sacked, I will make you take responsibility as general. You are an adult with a job now; this is what it's like." In other words: *Run away and you're dead.*

Even if I stayed at the fort, I'd die in battle eventually. And if I fled, I'd be executed. There I was, knee-deep in the most hopeless of situations.

"Answer me. You're a mere vassal of mine—as the ruler's younger brother, you have certain obligations. You must fight with your life to defend the domain our father left us."

Indeed, it was my duty to protect Nayvil. I had to protect our people and our land with my life. That was a ruling family's job.

Yeah, I'll do it. And I'm gonna survive, too.

"Understood. I will go to Nagraad at once."

When I returned to my manor, Laviala immediately lost her temper over my brother's treatment of me.

"This is just too cruel! 'Go to Fort Nagraad'… Really?! It's as if he's *trying* to have you killed!"

"I've got no choice. There's no denying the fort needs defending, and it's a fact that someone close to the ruler would raise morale."

"In that case, he should go himself! The only reason he doesn't is because he's afraid of battle! Besides, if the fort falls, then all of Nayvil will be in danger!"

Well, she wasn't wrong. I'd said too much to my stupid brother and turned his anger on me. He was being a real dumbass, so I couldn't help giving it back to him.

"Why don't you just defect to Mineria?" I could tell from the look in her eyes that Laviala was serious. Still—that was a very risky thing to discuss.

"Hey… What would we do if my brother had a spy in here?!"

"A lord's compassion is what earns him the love of his vassals. If he's cruel and nasty, they have every right to turn their back on him. Besides, it's the Hundred Years' Rebellion—betrayal happens all the time!"

Laviala was desperate to keep me alive. That was just how intense the fighting at Nagraad was. The fort was built upon a terrace right next to a river, making it tough to carry out an assault; however, with repeated onslaughts, it could fall at any time.

© Kaito Shibano

"Dying out there would serve no purpose whatsoever! Besides, if the lord of Nayvil's brother defected, I'm sure Mineria could spread the news to undermine him! You could even rule Nayvil as a vassal of Mineria—it wouldn't be out of the question!" Her argument was certainly persuasive enough. I couldn't deny that if I orchestrated things just right, I could actually improve my social standing from this.

It was then that my younger sister, Altia, tottered into the room. "Welcome home, Brother..." Not a moment after greeting me, she went into a coughing fit. She'd been sickly for years.

"Altia, if you're not feeling well, don't strain yourself just to come out and see me."

"But I heard talk of going to a fort... That means I won't be able to see you for a while..."

I sighed. "Laviala, scratch the betrayal plan. I can't take Altia with me. If I defected, she'd be—"

"That's true... He would make an example of Lady Altia..."

Geisel must have known from the start I couldn't betray him. I didn't have it in me to put Altia in danger. Besides, taking my sickly sister to a filthy fort wouldn't be much different from locking her in a burning mansion. And if anyone asked, I wouldn't be able to justify bringing my civilian sister along in the first place. I'd be a fool to think none of my brother's lackeys would be at the fort; if I did anything suspicious, it'd surely be reported up the ranks immediately.

"Guess I just have to go. I'll go, and I'll win this thing."

"But there can't be more than two hundred and fifty men in the fort...," said Laviala. "The enemy must number about two thousand... You can probably raise about a hundred yourself, but either way, it doesn't look good..."

Generally the attackers needed about triple the number of defenders in a siege, while conversely, you'd want about seven hundred soldiers to defend against two thousand attackers. Even then, multiplying the number of soldiers would be detrimental for sanitation, risking outbreak of disease and requiring a far greater food supply. In other words, it'd be better to defend with a small group of select troops if possible.

The problem was that defending with small numbers meant everyone was always stretched to their limit. Extended hostilities under extreme stress were essentially not sustainable. If the enemy caught you off guard for just a moment, you could get totally destroyed. At the very least, there was no way you could drive the enemy back.

"Even so, I just have to do this. It's my duty."

Let's pray this Oda Nobunaga job is insanely powerful...

◇

One hundred and twenty soldiers, led by Laviala and me, made their way toward Fort Nagraad. It rested on top of a low hill on our side of the river separating us from Mineria.

The defenders' morale did temporarily improve upon my arrival. They seemed to realize they hadn't been abandoned. This was a very important point, since soldiers tended to desert or defect when they thought they were being sacrificed. Nobody was really happy to die.

Of course, the enemy was always attacking some point or another, so no one could tell what would happen. But never mind that—there were rumors the opposition would soon unleash a full-scale assault.

I spoke in private with Kivik Klute, the commander who'd been holding down the fort. Though an old man with a completely white beard, he was certainly a capable individual, having protected the fort for so long. For generations, the head of the Klute family had used the name Kivik, and the present head was no exception.

"Actually, the enemy's sappers have built a path up to our fort... I do think they will make an all-out attack before long. I don't know when that will be, though."

"When that happens, will the fort hold?"

"The fort itself is sturdy. That's how we've held out for so long. However, the men are all exhausted. If the gate is breached just once, then..."

The situation was worse than I'd thought. In fact, that must've been why I'd been brought in. If the fort survived longer because of me, then great, and if I died, my brother would still be pleased. I had to survive this, if only to get revenge on him.

That night:

"The enemy is attacking!"

I sprang awake to someone shouting. So the enemy meant to take the fort in one go after all. To think we'd be attacked the first day I was here... Things just got worse and worse.

But then something that absolutely should never happen happened.

"The gate's open!"

"Where's the gate bar?!"

"Even the fittings are gone!"

I heard cries of dismay. The gate was unusable and wide open—we had a turncoat among our ranks. There was no other explanation. This was no longer a siege; we had no choice but to drive out the enemy.

"Laviala, stay close to me! We need to see what we're up against first!"

"Yes! I'll use the healing magic I learned from my mother, so you stay close, too!"

Laviala was born just a bit earlier than I was, so she was old enough to receive a profession, but she hadn't gone to the temple yet. She must've been avoiding coming of age before me, her master. That was probably why she hadn't married yet, either, despite being of marriageable age.

Still, even without a profession, Laviala was already more than capable. She'd learned how to use magic on her own. Many elves were skilled in the arcane arts. She was also quite proficient with a bow. Laviala might've even wanted to live her life as a warrior. It wasn't that uncommon for a woman.

A whole slew of enemies had already breached the fort. The crests on their armor were plainly that of our neighbor Mineria.

"They're already here," I said. "I doubt this is their full army, but there must be at least five hundred of them."

"Five hundred?! We can't win against those numbers!"

Some of the enemies had received cuts from our side, perhaps by wind magic, but it was too little against too many. With the attack coming at night, our soldiers' movements were slower, too. If only we had a Spell-sword, someone who could slay enemy after enemy single-handedly and give us the breakthrough we needed, but that was just something from war stories. It was plain as day that the fort was about to fall.

Commander Kivik came over to me, an arrow sticking out of his leather armor. "I'm sorry to say this is it. Nothing left but to fight to the death…"

He was right—too late for a retreat.

What a disappointing life this had been. Not even a month had passed since I'd become an adult. It was so anticlimactic, I didn't even feel sad. Now you see why I hated being the second son of some measly feudal lord.

I'd at least like Laviala to escape.

"Laviala, get out of here! You'll be fine on your own. And don't get caught by one of the male soldiers—you're too cute for that!"

"Is this really the time to be telling me I'm cute?!" cried Laviala. But she still hadn't given up. "I'm going to fight. It's my job to serve you!"

"Well then, how am I supposed to save you?!"

"Drive all the enemies away," Laviala responded slyly.

Like that's gonna happen. What a joke.

But at that moment…

…I wasn't sure why, but I felt a sort of confidence well up within me.

——You can overcome this. You see, concealed in your profession is the potential to become a conqueror.

I thought I heard something like an inner voice.

No way… Is my Oda Nobunaga job seriously that powerful?

I drew my sword. I didn't have time to waste on putting on heavy armor, but I was lighter that way. "Laviala—I'm going to protect you. Watch this."

"Y-yes, sir…! That's the Alsrod I know!" For a moment, Laviala was too stunned to say more, but she flashed me a smile.

I'd practiced my swordplay well enough. I wasn't going down so easily. I leaped into the fray. In that instant, I heard that inner voice again.

Special ability Conqueror's Might activated.
Physical ability doubled when in battle.

What's this voice? Did I gain some new ability?

I'd heard that people got new abilities when they mastered their profession. But I'd never heard of a voice echoing inside your head. Besides, doubled physical ability was just ludicrous. That was enough to make an ordinary man into a superhuman.

But all I could do was believe what the voice told me.

Don't let me down, Oda Nobunaga!

My body really did move like you wouldn't believe. Whether my opponents wore leather armor or iron, I pinpointed the gaps in their defenses and skewered one after another. My movements were perfectly precise. I was clearly moving of my own will, but it was as if it were someone else's body. My heart must not have caught up yet with my profession's new capabilities. I'd never experienced this kind of fighting, after all.

I cut down ten soldiers one at a time; as a result, our surroundings became that much safer.

"Lord Alsrod, were you always this good with a sword…?"

"I can't believe it, either, but I'm just gonna dive right in! I'm off to the front line!" I went on ahead, with faith that Oda Nobunaga could be just as good as Spellsword.

There were enemies everywhere, all hell-bent on bringing down the fort. But they were all simply too slow; I didn't feel in danger of getting hit at all.

——Of course they're too slow. Only a conqueror can stop a conqueror. Like that damn Akechi Mitsuhide, who took over my country—granted, his reign was short-lived. I only know of his downfall because it happened before I'd even made it to the afterlife.

There it was again. The voice had to be related to my profession some-how. It didn't seem as if it was going to possess me or anything, though, so that was neither here nor there. Was it the name of a hero from some other world? I was starting to make sense of it.

Whatever. All I need to do right now is get out of here alive.

I went beside Laviala and patted her shoulder in encouragement.

"Wait here. I'm going out. No matter what happens, I will be back."

"Y-yes, sir…" Laviala seemed to hesitate just a bit, but she agreed. She probably wanted to fight by my side for longer.

Sorry—just wait for me.

There was a saying that offense was the best defense. I plunged into a group running up the stairs to the gate, cutting down one after another. The bodies of the fallen knocked over more behind them.

Excellent, they're falling like an avalanche. I must've killed at least fifty already. Just a little more of that and they should start to turn tail. Once I convince them they don't have a chance, I win. Even if I have to kill another hundred, at this rate, I might actually be able to do just that.

There wasn't a weary bone in my body. "I'll slay anyone who approaches the gate! All of you, wipe out the ones who got into the fort!" Even the men ready to flee were reinvigorated by my call.

"That's right—we got this!"

"Lord Alsrod is with us!"

All right, make me proud. Unless more of them arrive, we should be able to mop them up.

I kept slaughtering the invaders in front of the gate. They were com-ing up the stairs, so I kicked them down here and there.

"He fights like a brute!" Unable to get through, they began to hurl insults.

A brute? Like I give a damn. I wasn't aware there were rules in a fight to the death. You were the ones who made one of our men betray his companions.

I heard the sound of the gate closing behind me. Our men must have fixed it. All that was left was to clean up the group in front of me, and the crisis would be over for now. I plunged into them.

I'd show them the power of my profession. I knew exactly where to thrust my sword to kill them.

Out of my way, you bastards. I'm the descendant of a viscount—no, the successor to the Conqueror's Might!

Their cries of horror went on—and on. After every swing of my sword, a spray of blood soon followed. When a mage tried to throw a fireball, I closed in and ran him through instead. As a spearman tried to jab at me, I jumped onto his spear and sliced off his head as I dismounted. The tide of battle was turning bit by bit from my work alone.

This would certainly drive them off, at least. I didn't fully understand it, but this was definitely thanks to my profession. Otherwise, I'd have died having killed only twenty of them, at most.

I'd made it to the foot of the hill. The enemy had largely already begun to retreat, so getting back to the fort seemed possible. However, upon climbing back to where I could see the fort, I heard a familiar voice.

"I—I can still fight! I can...s-still "

Laviala was fighting outside the gate. Her clothes were torn, and she was surrounded by enemies. Despite her skill with a bow, she'd come out to fight on the front lines.

"Lord Alsrod, I'm coming to your aid..."

That fool! I told her to wait at the fort! And she told me she would!

"I, Laviala Aweyu, refuse to let you die alone, Lord Alsrod!"

Ah, so she does *think I mean to die here. I was serious when I said I'd make it back and save her.*

It made sense, though. After all, she'd been by my side from the time I was born. It must have been natural for her to think we'd die together, too.

But I'm not gonna die out here, so neither should you.

I gripped my sword and dived in with all my might. "Don't you touch her!"

Before they could get her...

...I swung my sword without a moment's hesitation.

Special ability Conqueror's Pride activated.
When attempting to protect your own property, attack power doubles on top of Conqueror's Might.

Doubles...? Looks like I've got another unbelievably powerful ability...
I'd practiced my swordplay well enough, but to have quadruple my normal skill...?
My sword is glowing red from all the power, I thought as the enemy in front of me was bisected at the torso. The lower half, now supporting nothing, fell over slowly.

"Damn, quadruple strength is insane..."

The remaining foes couldn't disguise the fear coming over their faces. Our victory was practically sealed, but to protect Laviala, I was prepared for anything.

"Aaaah... H-he's a monster—!"

He wasn't finished, but I helped him to the afterlife anyway.

I proceeded to hew through the last of them, and my blade seemed to dull a bit. The new special ability really didn't last long. Just one attack was plenty, though.

"Laviala, are you unhurt?"

"Lord Alsrod... I'm sorry. I was just so afraid to leave you on your own..."

"I'll lecture you later. I'm just glad you're all right." I gently put my arm around Laviala's back. It was warm. She was alive, all right. I'd succeeded in protecting her.

"I'm...so happy you're alive..." And yet *she* was happily crying that *I* was alive.

"Hey, hey, that's my line. You're the one who was in danger..."

"But you went out there all by yourself... I thought you were going to be killed... I was so, so worried..."

Really, anyone would think as Laviala had. Berating her any more would be too harsh. Besides, I wanted to show her a smile, not scold her. She'd managed to escape from the jaws of death, after all.

"Sorry. When you've had some rest, use some of your healing magic on me." I patted her back.

Hmm, but that special ability just now had the words "When attempting to protect your own property" running through my mind… Huh, so for me, Laviala is my childhood friend and therefore my property…

I felt strangely embarrassed, so to hide it, I hugged her tighter than before.

"Lord Alsrod, that hurts."

"I don't want to lose you."

"You know I'm not going anywhere."

I hoped those words would prove true.

"Even if you do, I'll be bringing you back, you hear?"

Laviala and I returned to the fort triumphantly. The opposition was gone, and the fever pitch of battle had passed.

"We sent those Minerian bastards packing! Their bodies are all the way up to the fort!" My comrades' voices boomed out as I raised my sword. We didn't have time to get too relaxed, though. I needed to consult Commander Kivik about what was to come.

The commander bowed low before approaching me.

"I will notify the viscount at Nayvil Castle of your success at once. All the men here are witness to it!"

"No, we can't be sure how things would've gone with me alone. This victory belongs to everyone."

"The enemy has been positively eradicated. We are currently dumping the bodies into the river before they rot." The precipice behind the fort adjoined the river, conveniently enough.

"Thank you, commander. I was just wanting to speak with you about what we do next."

"You are the real commander. Please just call me Kivik."

"Sure, Kivik. Let's start the war council."

Kivik and I, together with Laviala, spoke alone in the fort's innermost chamber.

"We managed to defend ourselves, but we're not truly out of danger yet," I explained. "In fact, we're in trouble if we can't take the fight to them."

A wide river ran between Nayvil and Mineria. The current itself wasn't that fast, but the eastern shore—where our fort lay—formed a large terrace. The hills on the other side were smaller and gentle.

"The enemy is building their own fort on the opposite shore; if we don't evict them, it doesn't bode well for us…" Kivik brought his finger down on the map. This man was a seasoned leader; his claims had to be true.

Indeed, if that many enemy troops were stationed on the other shore, we'd have a perpetual crisis on our hands.

Laviala looked perplexed as she stared at the river area on the map. She seemed to be trying to work out a plan. Laviala had always enjoyed strategizing.

"Why don't we attack them at night?" she suggested. "The sound of the river should mask our troops' footsteps, so I don't think the enemy would hear our approach."

Interesting. So we'd be giving them a taste of their own medicine. Still—

"I'm afraid we don't have enough troops to capture the fort…," Kivik lamented.

The enemy, like us, would want to protect the fort they built. It would be too small to house all their troops inside, but still, their ability to attack us long-term was thanks to that foothold. Their troops who didn't fit into the fort must have been recruited as additional attack troops.

"If we could just land a good hit or perhaps create an unfavorable situation for them…," Laviala went on. "But I just can't come up with anything."

Even Laviala's smarts seemed like no match for this. However, once again I thought I heard a voice in my head.

——Fear not. You have access to my experiences.

The strangest idea just came to me.

I wasn't sure whether I could make it work, but with a few sappers at my command, I could sure give it a shot.

"I just had a great—no, an ingenious—idea."

*　　*　　*

I glanced at Laviala and then Kivik.

"Listen," I said to them. "I'm gonna make something that's such a pain in the ass it'll drive the enemy crazy."

Their reaction was better than I'd expected. I'd thought for sure they would say it was ridiculous or couldn't be done.

"If we don't at least try something so unexpected, we'll never turn the tables. Let's do it!" Kivik shouted jovially.

◇

We executed the plan two days later, at night, crossing the river when our foes were asleep. They'd notice us if we were to ambush them right then and there, but we weren't going to do that. Our destination was the hill on the north side of their fort.

We got there safely and got straight to digging. In particular we built a wall into our south side—where the enemy would attack from—to prevent our opponent's advance. If they did attack, I planned to have archers shoot them from high up, but there was no movement from them.

"Listen, everyone! We're in a race against time! If we're not mostly done by morning, this'll all be for nothing! I'm giving all the directions here! I want your absolute trust!"

The men toiled with all their might. Honestly, they were working more diligently than I'd expected, probably because I'd gone out to the front line in the battle two days prior. The surviving troops were prepared to die for me.

Up until then, the only person I'd ever felt I could count on was Laviala, whom I'd grown up with. My brother looked down on me and had never even given me a proper army, so I'd been worried about how effectively I could even command… Maybe I had a gift for leadership.

Or perhaps my success here, too, was because of that mysterious Oda Nobunaga job? Assuming Oda Nobunaga was the name of some hero, maybe I had the charisma of a hero in me, too. But I needed to worry about that later; there was so much to do.

Dawn finally arrived; the sky began to brighten.

"Thanks, everyone. We made it in time."

On the enemy fort's north side, our dirt fort had been made ready in just one night. Yes, that was what my plan had been. With a fort next to theirs, we could garrison troops right there. The enemy couldn't let their guard down, and above all, they had our fort on their land now. There was no way they could let that stand.

Still, we couldn't get complacent. They might come attack us right away. Besides, the fort had been constructed hastily. We'd made dirt ramparts for an efficient defense with bows and spears, but many parts of it weren't finished; even after daybreak we needed to keep working.

——Well done. Now, this is a plan I would think of. By building a fort on their territory in one day, you can crush your opponents' morale and sow confusion. Use this power to your heart's content.

I heard the voice again. I tried asking a question back.

Hey, are you Oda Nobunaga? Some kinda hero?

——Indeed, Oda Nobunaga was once the name of a conqueror, but now it's nothing more than the name of a job. However, since you have what it takes to follow in those footsteps, I'm merely lending you my power as your profession. Be at ease, for I have neither the right nor the power to manipulate you. I suppose you could say this is just my way of passing the time.

I got a response back.

Talking with my profession? What the hell? Pretty unorthodox, if you ask me, but I'll just take his word for it. Even if I don't, there's no way to get rid of a suitable profession anyway.

If he was an evil spirit, there'd be no way to counter him, and if he was an evil spirit that rescued me from death, I'd happily be his follower.

© Kaito Shibano

——I, too, was mocked as a fool in my youth. But I still took control of the country. You can do that, too.

Guess I just have to believe him.

A panicked soldier brought me the news: The enemy was on the attack. I'd expected as much.

"All right, fight with your lives, gentlemen! The enemy is scared! We can win this!"

The men whooped energetically at my call. We were all in this together, no doubt about it. There was no way we could lose if our enemies were attacking us, without a plan, simply for being there.

"Leave them to me!" Laviala yelled. She took cover behind a small rampart jutting out from the fort and, raising her head, unleashed a flurry of arrows. The enemy soldiers who got hit went down.

Laviala's bow technique was quite good; lots of elves were highly adept at archery. As for the enemy soldiers, their arrows were bouncing off the rampart, unable to reach her.

We'd fashioned the fort to naturally lead attackers to the front, but since we'd made it too steep to climb, our assailants became target practice for our bows. Whether they shot arrows or magic fireballs, they didn't have the power to break down the walls. This fort was made entirely of dirt. It couldn't be burned down. It couldn't be dismantled. There wasn't even a gate to pry open. It was exceedingly simple. This was the most that could be built in a night, but because it was so simple, our foes were at a loss.

The opposing forces started attacking again once they finally realized there was a way up to the fort on the flank. But that was also according to plan. We'd deliberately made the path sloped, narrow, and zigzag. When trying to break through, they would inevitably get slowed down where the path bent, resulting in a bottleneck. That was when we'd fell them from above with arrows.

"Shoot them all! This path only leaves them more vulnerable! They're fish in a barrel!"

The first ten who came up all perished immediately. We could see everything the attackers were doing from our position. What's more, the path was too narrow for the enemy to break through by relying on numbers alone. We could pick them all off when they were coming single file.

"I was worried whether a dirt fort like this would be effective, but it seems to do the job," the veteran commander Kivik said, astonished.

"It was just a hunch I had," I replied.

When we'd been strategizing, for whatever reason all I could think of was a world where everyone was fighting with dirt forts. It might've come from the knowledge or experience of Oda Nobunaga. In that world, merely by creating a difference in elevation with dirt, the forts could easily fend off their attackers. Even a hundred men could repel a thousand without much trouble.

Indeed, since no enemy soldier could fly, even dirt could be made into as vexing a fort as any, with the right handiwork. A castle, after all, was only ever a place to have a superior vantage point over an opponent. If you had the time, it was great to make a stone castle, but a defensive point could be made without it.

With a suicidal push, some of the enemy had finally made it up the sloped path and were trying to get into the fort itself. They certainly were audacious.

Crossing no-man's-land to get at us? I'll take you up on that.

However, they all quickly turned pale. The way they'd come didn't lead to the fort.

A great, deep trench lay in between; not even the strongest leap could carry them across it.

——Ah, so you have a moat. Cut off a man's path forward with that, and you'll stop him dead in his tracks.

There was Oda Nobunaga at it again with the commentary. Maybe he liked to talk.

Laviala shot the soldiers who had been stopped. Unlike my foes, I could move my troops around using wood planks.

"This dirt fort seems simplistic, but it's actually really sophisticated. I'm shocked," Laviala mused.

"Yeah, so am I. Just by messing with their path in, we can get this much of an edge."

"As long as they keep coming at us so naively, we can't lose. I mean, all our men are still in good shape." Laviala looked behind her. She was right; there was hardly an injured one among them.

We were fighting from an overwhelmingly superior position, so we had almost no fear of death or even any real danger. On the other hand, the enemy probably already had over a hundred casualties. Those who came from the front got shot up, and the ones who tried to invade up the slope were destroyed piecemeal.

None of them had expected us to have a fort all the way out here. If they were only going to rush in without thinking, they were just going to raise their body count. They clearly hadn't devised even the slightest plan for capturing the fort.

In the end, the enemy withdrew, having accomplished virtually nothing. They seemed to have finally given up taking the fort.

"Shall we give chase?" Kivik asked. *Well, it is a chance to beat them up even more...*

"No, it's fine. We don't have as many troops as they do. Going out would only work in their favor."

We celebrated our win with a victory cheer.

"Sure, I was the one who thought of this plan. But without all your courage, it never could have happened. You have my gratitude!"

At my words, the men came alive, with the cry "Long live the Nayvils!" reverberating across the land.

Hearing that we'd gained the upper hand, my brother sent us reinforcements. With those, we could protect both Fort Nagraad and the one on the other shore. In a letter, my brother praised my building a fort on the enemy's land, saying, "I cannot express what an accomplishment this is."

He may not have been happy I was having success, but he was undoubtedly pleased about the threat being largely mitigated.

With Mineria apparently having to give up on taking us by storm, the tense war situation cooled off for a bit. The enemy had lost too many men. They surely had no choice but to go back to the drawing board.

I received an order from my brother to return home. Understandable— I was only ever supposed to be emergency help, after all. I would return to my land with Laviala.

"Salute Lord Alsrod!" Kivik had all the men salute me before I went.

"You are a hero for the ages, Lord Alsrod! Nayvil has been saved thanks to you!"

"If I'm a hero, then so is each and every one of you! Let's fight for Nayvil with our heads held high!" I replied somewhat loftily before departing.

On the road home, Laviala said to me, "I thought I knew everything about you, but your achievements exceeded my expectations three times over."

"I can't argue. I exceeded my own expectations three times over." I'd gone into battle prepared to die, but we'd managed to drive the enemy back.

Apparently, Laviala wasn't satisfied, though; she was putting out her cheeks cutely. It meant she was pouting.

"Is something wrong?"

"You should have told me you had such incredible powers! Hiding things from me is just cruel!"

"Like I said, I had no idea myself! What do you want me to do? Personally, I think it's all thanks to my job."

"You mean that Oda Nobunaga thing?"

"Exactly." I nodded from atop my horse. "Who cares about Spellswords? This has to be the strongest profession there is!"

"First, I would like to sincerely apologize for ridiculing your profession... Even ignoring the assistance you received from your powers, you fulfilled your duty admirably. W-without a doubt, this is the greatest thing anyone in our clan has accomplished... It's—it's incredible..."

Just as I'd thought, Geisel wasn't smiling when we met again at Nayvil Castle. That was what happened when someone you belittled suddenly turned the tides. Only a fool made fun of someone who wasn't actually a joke after all. In short, my brother's pride was hurt. Well, he got his just deserts.

Since there was no point in making him angry, I decided to act humble for now. "My lord, it was you who moved to send your brother to the fort in crisis. Your flawless calculation is to thank here. Doubtless you would have the praise of our late father, as well."

"I —I see... Well, I guess you're right..."

That was all it took to improve his mood. If he was this naive, any conniving vassals of his must've had it easy.

"In any case, I must reward you for your accomplishments. Until now, I've only granted you about half of the small village Hardt. I shall give you the entire village and its neighboring ones, making you the lord of three villages in total. I shall also grant you the title of baron. Call yourself the Baron of Hardt, after the village."

"Thank you, my lord. I shall fight more than ever for the sake of Nayvil."

Unlike that of a viscount, a baron title could not be inherited, so it was no problem to give it out like candy as a reward. Also, since the Nayvils were a line of viscounts, it was impossible to give out the same viscount title anyway.

The Viscount of Nayvil himself was only a small lord with the land of about a county and a half.

He was just a puny rural noble with the same county's worth of land that plenty of others like him in the country had.

The Kingdom of Therwil was divided into sixty administrative units called prefectures, each containing ten or so counties. However, that number varied widely depending on the size of the prefecture itself. I was an inhabitant of Nayvil County in Fordoneria Prefecture.

The voice in my head calling himself Oda Nobunaga had also said, *"Ah, so the prefectures of this world correspond to provinces, like Owari, Mino, and Mikawa, and counties are the same as Japan's districts. This Nayvil clan would be like a local samurai lord holding just over one of Owari's districts. Compared to my grandfather Nobusada's time, I'm not sure which would be bigger. My father took half of Owari himself."*

I didn't really know what he was talking about, but apparently Oda Nobunaga's father had control of half a prefecture, in which case he was big enough to call himself a count. That made for a fairly powerful family in its own right.

Traditionally, a lord possessing more than half a prefecture held the title of count. On the other hand, a lord holding less than that could be no higher than a viscount. If a smallish viscount were to try to call himself a count, everyone around him would put pressure on him until he learned his place. So while I wouldn't say a sneeze would topple our clan, the power of the Viscount of Nayvil could be wiped out at any time.

Seeing my brother relaxing on his throne, I sighed to myself. To be honest, I wanted to oust my brother and take his position as viscount right away. True, I despised him, but the real problem was that a second-rate lord like him would give me orders like defending that fort, putting my life in danger. However, starting a rebellion now and winning was pretty much impossible, by any calculation. I didn't even have a righteous cause.

——Don't rush it. To become a conqueror, first you must prepare. Taking your first prefecture is rather painstaking, but turning five into ten is simple. The time will come. I didn't conquer all of Owari until a while after I'd defeated Imagawa Yoshimoto.

If my inner voice says it, I'll believe it. Who knows what all those names are, though.

——I didn't take Inuyama Castle in a day, you know. Of course, once I had driven out Imagawa, my domination was practically sealed.

Other world or not, it was nice to have someone experienced on your side. Still, I was ages away from unifying Fordoneria Prefecture; I wasn't even an independent lord yet.

——Indeed, you are still but a mere babe among your fellow clansmen.

This inner voice could be a bit rude on occasion, though. Oh well. Better than an evil spirit that steals your soul.

With the meeting with my brother over, I set out to manage the new land I'd just acquired. Even with just three villages, I had an important role in the Nayvil family. Returning to my manor, I first visited Altia's room.

"Brother! I thought I'd never see you again…!" she sobbed as soon as she saw me.

"Aw, c'mon, have a little faith in me!"

"But it was such a lost cause…"

She wasn't wrong there. That bridge was incredibly dangerous, and I'd crossed it.

"I think you should be able to rest a bit more easily from now on." I stroked Altia's head.

"Yes, Brother..."

She smiled faintly. If our mother had been of a higher social standing and Altia had been healthy, Altia probably would have been used in a political marriage by now. Ironically, the reason she and I could even stay together was because of her unfortunate lot in life. Our mother had been nothing more than the daughter of a Nayvil merchant. She'd been our father's concubine because of her good looks, but I could scarcely remember her face, since she'd passed away giving birth to Altia.

I wished I could move somewhere more hospitable for my sister's sake, with her being so sick. Or maybe I really could? I had the rank for it now.

I requested permission to construct a new home, emphasizing the need for my sister's rehabilitation. My brother approved it without a fuss: "Make yourself a house fit for a baron." Indeed, because my rank had gone up, there was no reason I couldn't set up a residence befitting my social status.

I put my new home on the village high ground. My local reputation had risen dramatically, so the construction went extremely smoothly.

By changing location, I was able to greatly improve my defensive capability. If push came to shove, I could fight while barricaded in there.

The dry, refreshing breeze that blew through the new building made Altia happy. Her condition seemed to have improved, too. My inner voice chimed in: *"I also frequently relocated my castle. Nothing wrong with that. Do it as much as you can."* Always nice to have his support, too.

Another bit of good news came around the time the building was completed. The veteran commander Kivik, who'd defended Fort Nagraad with me, visited me at my home.

"With the fort stabilized, another person took my place, and so I have returned."

"It's been a while since we last met, Commander. It's good to see you again."

"Also, if possible, I would like to serve as your aide." Ultimately,

Kivik was a servant of the lord of the domain. I was merely a vassal serving the same lord, so it was impossible for him to serve me. Thus, in the form of an aide, he wanted the role of assisting me.

"Very well—that's fine by me. Make the request to my brother yourself."

"Yes, sir! Thank you very much! These old bones are prepared to die for you!"

The approval came without incident, and Kivik effectively became my vassal. That served to boost my reputation even more. Having protected that fort for so long, he was highly popular. Other long-serving officers and the like started coming to me as a result. Apparently, people who were fans of military prowess had gotten the impression that there was value in serving me.

More and more swordsmen living nearby wanted to become my servants as well. Those who didn't directly serve the lord of the domain could be integrated as vassals without issue.

Also, thanks to my connection with Laviala, her relatives and other elves came to serve as retainers. It seemed that after hearing of my successes, they thought I could help them, too.

The support of the elf clan Laviala's mother belonged to was particularly important, as the other elves then followed suit. Practically all the elven forces in the county were under my command.

"The little things pile up, don't they?" I said to Laviala one day while compiling a military register. Yet more elves had joined my ranks, and I had to revise the register each time. Not a bad problem to have, honestly.

"You have an appeal that's never been seen in Nayvil. Everyone believes you can do something for them," Laviala replied as she helped me. I couldn't hire real civil officials at my rank, so for clerical work I had to enlist the help of trusted companions.

"I'm gonna ignore most of that, since you're always complimenting me."

"Oh, come on, Lord Alsrod... But truly, I feel you possess a sort of innate charisma." Maybe that was thanks to Oda Nobunaga, after all.

Within the Nayvil domain, my forces had arguably grown to be second only to that of the ruler, my brother Geisel.

◇

The other day, when I received my brother as a guest during his hunting trip, he looked quite tense—must've been the number of vassals I had.

"So, Brother...why do you have so many vassals...?"

"It's all because of our great victory at Fort Nagraad. Skilled fighters from the surrounding lands came to me seeking work, and the result is what you see."

"D-don't you find it difficult taking care of such a large number...?"

"Indeed. But because the population has grown, fields that had lain fallow can be used again, so my estate's harvest will increase. I have been able to apportion land to my new vassals, too."

In this age, plenty of land was still left neglected due to a shortage of workers. I'd wasted no time turning it back into fields, which wasn't difficult once the worker problem was solved. After all, the name Nayvil itself meant *beautiful farmland*.

"I—I see... Still, you yourself are just another one of my own vassals... M-make sure you don't forget your place..."

Say whatever you want. I'll never commit to that.

"Nevertheless, much of the fort's prior defense was fraught with danger," I replied. "It would have been far easier to slay the scores of enemy soldiers if I'd had the manpower I do now. These forces will undoubtedly be necessary for Nayvil. Please do understand."

"Er... I see... Good point... All right, keep up the good work..."

"Yes, sir. I think our father would be smiling from heaven to see me assisting you."

Being in a better position now, I was more articulate than I used to be. I was going to keep driving him all the way into a corner. Of course... if I kept this up, my paranoid brother would probably make a move sooner or later. With this knowledge in mind, before Geisel could try anything, I had my sources look into what he thought of me.

My answer came in no time. A spy who'd been disguised as a peddler at Nayvil Castle gave their report.

"Lord Geisel appears to be quite afraid of you. He seems to be worried about being killed for his title, especially because he has no children yet."

"I see. I knew as much, but I guess he really can't hide his feelings."

It'd been only about nine months since I'd returned from the fort, meaning not even a year had passed since I'd received my profession and officially become an adult. I certainly had never thought things would change this much.

It was common for famous warriors to establish independent dynasties. People flocked to those with power. On the other hand, it was inherently harder for my brother, who was inept at war, to earn people's confidence.

In this age, lords great and small all ruled with military regimes. Thus, the ones who weren't skilled in the ways of combat were seen as unable to protect others. Of course, the people would be thrilled if war could be avoided with diplomacy, but I knew more than anyone that my brother had no such skill.

"I'll send my brother's wife a safe-childbirth talisman from a prominent temple. Keep up the intel gathering."

The merchant spy went on their way.

I wasn't really doing anything too suspicious, so my brother couldn't confiscate my land or punish me. He'd most likely try to kill me before long; he couldn't just patiently wait for me to rise in power. That moment would be an enormous opportunity, though. I'd bolster my reputation as much as possible before then.

I took it upon myself to maintain the family tombs. As a bona fide member of the clan, I was allowed to clean the graves by law. But from the outside, it would look as if I were the successor of the Nayvil family. Of course, ostensibly I was acting as a stand-in for the busy family head.

On one such occasion, my inner voice spoke to me.

——You should try to promote economic development while you can. There's no such thing as a poor conqueror, after all. Try it out somewhere small first.

*　　*　　*

A little income never hurt anyone. But what exactly should I do?

——Remove the shop tax. The market on the main road will grow larger.

Everyone had always known you had to pay a tax when opening a shop at the market, though it wasn't necessary to pay dues to a trade guild, as it was at the Nayvil Castle town.

Then how would the ruler earn anything from it?

——Change the system so part of profits must be paid.

Wouldn't they just run off without paying?

——As long as they're making money, the merchants will comply. They wouldn't want to ruin a good thing by being stingy. There's no harm done if one or two people don't make enough money to pay. Better to collect taxes from where the money is.

I decided to go ahead and believe him.

I sent a declaration throughout my lands, saying, "There will no longer be a tax on setting up shop in the market. Both merchants and farmers may sell whatever they like. Ten percent of profits must be paid, however."

The effect was immediate.

Upon inspecting the market on the main road, I could see it'd obviously grown larger in scale from before. As more people visited the market, others came to set up new ancillary businesses, such as selling alcohol or boxed meals. The growth of the market accelerated.

I went around with Laviala for another inspection about half a year after revising the market system.

"I remember this countryside market from when I was a little girl. To see it so lively now, it's like I'm dreaming."

"It's still small compared to the Nayvil Castle town, but it might be the largest makeshift market in all of Nayvil."

"The elves are selling medicinal herbs, and there are so many more animal people peddling than before. This is more than a highway market; it's almost a city!"

"More castle-town merchants are opening shop here, too. Since there's no setup costs, failure here isn't as much of a risk."

"It really is a huge success."

For the time being, the tax was coming in as expected, too. Since they would be stripped of their trade rights if they were caught breaking the law, the places with a profit made a sincere effort to pay. If anything, people probably would've paid money for the opportunity to sell there.

"But...this will provoke the viscount, won't it...?" Laviala asked, lowering her voice a bit.

"It certainly will."

My brother would come for me soon.

I began further investigations into the goings-on at my brother's residence, Nayvil Castle, which was located on a level plain and was surrounded by two moats. The castle town was reasonably well-to-do. When settling here, the Nayvil family took the name of the land as their own and ruled for many years.

The situation became clear sooner than I had expected. Once again, the spy disguised as a peddler gave me the details.

"Here is my report, sir. Lord Geisel is said to be devising a scheme to assassinate you. Specifically, he plans to feign illness and then summon you to take his place as ruler."

"I see. So it is true, then."

"What do you mean, sir...?" The spy was confounded by my attitude.

"I've already heard the same thing from another vassal I had at Nayvil Castle. It seems quite a few of my brother's henchmen are saying the plan is too rushed to work. That's how the information reached me in the first place."

Even a lackey couldn't go on serving a lord who collapsed at the drop of a hat. It just showed how much people were starting to lose faith in my brother. There were also many servants from my father's time who doubted my brother's abilities. Additionally, I'd managed to hear from old vassals who wanted to give their real opinions, something that made it even easier for them to clash with my brother. Of course, my brother was indeed incompetent, whether they realized it or not.

"Lord Alsrod, you were right not to go to Nayvil Castle after all," Laviala said, relieved.

"If nothing else, the thought of going to see him without bodyguards didn't feel right." Even before the assassination plot, I'd had my suspicions. He probably hated me more than ever for the commercial success of my market, too. Thus, I'd recently been avoiding going to Nayvil Castle.

I dismissed the spy. It was time for a strategy meeting—though it was just Laviala and I talking together. We had the relationship you'd expect of milk siblings raised by the same person, and she was my confidant among confidants. I went to her first when I wanted to speak my mind about something.

The room was dark, with just a lantern burning dimly.

"Feigning illness and assassinating you in the castle...? Really, what a convenient turn of events for us." Laviala laughed, undaunted.

We lived in a treacherous world; even Laviala wasn't just a sweet little girl.

"Honestly, I was thinking so, too. This way, we can have him die of 'illness' for real." If I killed my lord, I wouldn't be able to escape condemnation as a usurper. But if he spread news of his illness on his own, all I had to do was *see that through*.

"But still... As awful as he may be, it must be hard for you to have to kill your own brother..."

While it was true that we were related by blood, if I had too much sympathy for him now, I might end up being murdered instead.

——Precisely. Siblings or not, you must defeat your enemies. Otherwise you can never be a conqueror.

The voice was back.
Did you slay your kin, too?

——I killed my younger brother—although he'd tried to kill me first. Most people were on my brother Nobukatsu's side in the

beginning. Despite my smaller numbers, I crushed him and won their confidence.

Not too different from my situation, then. Except I, the younger brother, was the one doing the deed.

"It's fine, Laviala. Altia's the only family I've got anyway."

"I understand. I will also do everything in my power for you." The gallantry in Laviala's resolve just made her ten times as beautiful as always. That moment, my eyes happened to meet hers. Before I knew what I was doing, I put my hand to her face.

"Lord Alsrod…," Laviala said bashfully. I was surprised at what I was doing, myself, but it made me clearly aware of how I felt.

"You know… I intend to become the lord of Nayvil. I'm sorry, but I don't think there's any way I can make you my official wife. But… you're so…" Back when I rescued Laviala at the fort, I'd realized for the first time that I thought of Laviala as my own, and I wanted to make her more so. "I want you to be mine, even more than you already are."

Laviala nodded slowly as she smiled. "I've always believed I was destined to serve you, ever since the moment I was born. So this must be part of that destiny, too. Besides, you saved my life once."

That day, I made love to Laviala.

"Your chest is awfully flat."

"Don't say that… I can run much faster this way, which is perfect for an elf…"

"Sorry. Besides, I'm pretty much the only one who's seen under your clothes, right?"

Laviala was many things to me—my milk sister, my childhood friend, a part of my family, a vassal, a comrade in arms—but now she was also my lover. Good thing my enemy was planning to lure me out to him; that way, I didn't have to worry so much about prepping my house for defense.

◇

Official word of my brother Geisel's illness came from Nayvil Castle before long. Out of courtesy, I sent a messenger to offer condolences, but I never went myself. On the contrary, I carried out a plan to attract his disaffected vassals to my side. By that point, I'd arguably outstripped him in terms of sheer military power. After all, his forces consisted of only what he could gather from his vassals, and a portion of those vassals were on my side. And I had old pros like Kivik, who was known for his grit.

Eventually, I was notified that my brother's illness had not improved but had turned almost critical. I was ordered to come to the castle. Naturally, after summoning me, he planned to kill me.

"It's time."

I arrived at Nayvil Castle with five hundred soldiers, including Kivik. That wouldn't be a large number for a viscount to assemble, but for a baron underneath him it was. To tell the truth, I brought as many peasants as I could, too, even though they weren't so good at fighting.

I had a reason for making a show of numbers. My brother's men were flummoxed. Even if they'd expected a small escort, they certainly never would've thought I'd come with enough numbers for a military maneuver.

"Lord Alsrod, what in the world is the meaning of all these troops...?"

"It would be most shameful to bring only a small escort when succeeding my brother as viscount; that would bring disgrace upon him. For dignity's sake, I came with as many soldiers as I could muster."

"B-but..."

Just then Laviala came forward. She was by my side that day, as always. I didn't really want to involve her in the danger, but she said she was coming, and that was that. "Take a good look. These soldiers are in formal wear. They are here not for war, but to show the baron's authority."

"U-understood... However, they must all wait outside the moat..."

"No, these soldiers are the baron's escort," Laviala replied. "They will wait inside the moat, in front of the castle."

"Still, with this many men entering, if something were to happen—"

"How disrespectful! This is the man who will succeed the family throne: Lord Alsrod!" yelled Laviala.

They finally caved and opened the way. My five hundred men stopped right in front of the castle building. Surrounding myself with my most capable individuals, I proceeded into the castle. Perhaps my brother would think the assassination plan was impossible and give up; either way, as long as he relinquished control of Nayvil to me, that was all that mattered.

I'd already spread news of my brother's condition throughout the region. He'd informed me about it, so all I did was pass it on. If he handed over power without protest, with illness as reason, I had no problem letting him live in a sort of retirement. But it all depended on what turn of events would take place.

What's your move, brother? If you want to survive, abdicating and retiring someplace quiet is your only option.

Carefully, carefully, as slowly as possible, we advanced down the hallway.

My brother was a coward. He wouldn't have the assassination carried out in front of his own eyes. If I were to be attacked, it'd probably happen as I walked through the castle halls.

"There they are!" cried Laviala, swiftly throwing a knife toward the wall.

An assassin fell out from behind a pillar, pierced through the chest.

"My god—an assassin?! Could they be after my life?" I shouted theatrically. The assassins would have no choice but to come out now. My guide also tried to draw his sword, so I cut him down first.

Special ability Conqueror's Might activated.
Physical ability doubled when in battle.

Sorry, but I'm the better fighter!

In an instant, the scene turned into a melee, though I'd come with enough men to deal with it. We'd worn armor underneath our clothes, too, giving us an overwhelming advantage.

"Lord Alsrod, we're fine here! Make your way to Lord Geisel!" yelled Laviala as she fought back against the enemy. Indeed, if my brother got away, it'd cause a lot of trouble for me.

"Got it! But you come, too!"

"Huh…?"

"I'm stronger when I have you to protect!"

——That's it. That's the spirit of a conqueror. Now soldier on!

My inner voice had my back, too, though I'd do it even without being told. If I couldn't protect the one I loved, what was I even capable of?

Laviala and I ran toward my brother's living room. We were confronted by a few foes on the way, but they were no match for us.

Additional profession bonus from advancement: He Who Seizes Power, always active.
Enemies standing in your way are intimidated, reducing their abilities by twenty percent. However, confident enemies are unaffected.

Oh, so I get effects like this, too. Now even a Fighter's basic abilities will be no different from the average strong enemy's.

My opponents clearly withered when they came before me. They trembled, unable to even grip their weapons properly.

"Out of my way! Don't you know who I am?!"

Each swing of my sword flew like sparks as I lashed at my foes mercilessly.

I'd figured out the right way to use the Oda Nobunaga profession. The more I lived as a conqueror, the more this profession boosted my powers. My physical abilities at the moment clearly exceeded that of a simple soldier. Plus, I was trying to protect Laviala, so that special ability from before activated as well.

Special ability Conqueror's Pride activated.
When attempting to protect your own property, attack power doubles.

*　　*　　*

Laviala was mine through and through. I could now say that with my head held high.

My foes' weapons went flying as I struck with my sword at lightning speed. Another slash would slice their heads clean off.

I won't lose. I can't lose.

"There aren't many foes here, since your brother was only planning to assassinate you! Let's press on!" Laviala called.

"Yeah! And I'm not letting him escape, either!"

I'd already blocked off the rear exit with my troops, though he might've built other ways out. Or maybe he'd even disguise himself and try to leave through the front?

And so after slaying the two soldiers guarding my brother's room, I barged right in. He was trembling in bed, putting on a show of being ill.

"Brother, playing games isn't going to change anything."

"No... There's been some mistake... I don't know anything about this... I wasn't planning to assassinate you..."

——Groveling wretch! I want to wash out my ears just listening to him!

My inner voice howled indignantly. For a conqueror, a worm trying to save his neck at the gallows must have been the most unforgivable act of all.

"Then is it true you are ill?"

"Y-yes... I'll give you the Nayvil family domain here and now! From this moment, you are the ruler of Nayvil!"

"That is most generous of you. I humbly accept," I replied, kneeling before him. I knew he was holding a knife.

"Die, you bastard!!" he shouted as he swung the blade down. Scum to the very end.

So transparent. Some surprise attack this is!

I immediately ran him through the heart with my sword. "I'm viscount

49

now! Brother or not, treason against the viscount bears the death penalty!" This was the execution of a rebel—nothing more, nothing less.

My brother dropped the knife then and there. I'd snuffed out his life in a single stroke.

I'd been trying to give him a chance to make it out of this alive, but he hadn't even been capable of understanding that. It was a pity, but even if I hadn't killed him, he'd have died in disgrace somewhere else anyway.

"A beautifully executed attack, Lord Alsrod," said Laviala. "Or should I say Viscount?"

"Sounds about right. But my domain is just a county and a half; it's still too small. Ayles Caltis of Mineria controls a whole prefecture and has the title of count."

If we didn't expand, Nayvil couldn't be protected. Going about squashing neighbors of our own size seemed like a good idea.

Just then Kivik came in. Our enemies must have been suppressed, then.

"We killed all the assassins. I don't think there will be any more opposition."

"Got it. I'm done here, too. Tell the people we had a traitor in our midst and not to come near this room until we know it's safe."

Afterward, news spread throughout the land that Lord Geisel of Nayvil had relinquished power to Lord Alsrod of Hardt.

With the lot who supported my brother unable to say the illness was a hoax, the matter was settled. Even if they didn't feel like obeying, I could just put them down one by one. I'd have way less guilt about that than about killing my brother.

I openly took over as viscount. As celebration for the time being, I temporarily lowered taxes throughout the domain. With that, the masses would surely welcome me, too.

◇

Four days after the chaos had subsided, the cleaning of Nayvil Castle had been finished, and I returned.

We explained the commotion with the assassins by saying that men from another domain had been trying to wipe out the Nayvil clan and had been out to kill both my dying brother Geisel and myself. Nobody would have the courage to say it was I who'd killed Geisel while he was trying to make a surprise attack on me.

I sat on the viscount's throne, my new vassals all lined up below me. Among them were many of those who'd been working for me. Most of their faces were lit with excitement.

A new era was about to begin.

"I'm not just going to keep Nayvil as is; I'm going to expand it. More precisely, I'm going to be a conqueror."

Some were taken aback, whereas others began to snicker.

"Are you amused by the idea? I have all the makings of a conqueror. I began with only half a village to my name, and I've risen this far already. While my brother was alive, I came to be second in power only to him."

The people who'd thought I was joking looked sheepish. But I understood why they'd been snickering, so I wasn't angry.

"Take a good look. In no time, my land has grown tenfold."

Of course, a measly ten times wasn't what I had my sights on.

"I'm going to put an end to this Hundred Years' Rebellion era. I will build an era where this kingdom is no longer rife with conflict."

With my Oda Nobunaga job, this would turn out to be more than just some fairy tale.

After becoming lord of the domain, I was busy for a while with various duties.

First, because of the change of ruler, I had to send letters of territorial protection to my vassals and various institutions in the domain, such as temples. Since the promises of protection were all in the name of the previous lord, my brother, I had to reissue them all in my own. Really, I only had to check their contents, so it didn't require much thought.

But meeting with others inevitably takes time and energy. All manner of people came to pay respects to the new lord, so I had to receive them. I couldn't make everyone match their schedule to mine, and thoughtlessly sending an envoy would be rude.

Additionally, Laviala was always by my side as an adviser, so she was as exhausted as I was. "Ah, my neck is so stiff... Lord Alsrod..." She was constantly holding her neck. When we were alone, she was herself a bit more.

Incidentally, I hadn't made Laviala my official wife. Because of my status, it was crucial that I have a political marriage, so it would be a bad idea to openly hold a ceremony with her. Also, sadly, since Laviala was half-elven, if I announced her as my wife, some people would say it wasn't appropriate for someone of my status.

Still, no one would criticize a ruler for having several mistresses. Rather, since I was already eighteen years old, I couldn't afford to be childless for long. I wanted to have a child with Laviala as soon as possible.

"What other choice do we have? Boring work like this is a lord's job, too."

"I thought perhaps we'd live a bit more luxuriously than this now that you're a viscount, but I suppose it wasn't to be... Ah, I never thought my neck would be this stiff before I was twenty..."

"Let me massage it, then. It's just the two of us here, so I don't have to act like a viscount."

"Have *you* massage me, Lord Alsrod?! I couldn't!" She blushed and waved her hand. In a sense, she was my wife, but she never went beyond her place as my subject.

"Why act all shy if I'm offering? C'mon, lemme try." A bit forcibly, I put my hands on her shoulders. She was stiffer than I'd imagined. "How tense have you been, helping me with my work...?"

"We can never be sure some miscreants aren't lurking around to kill you... Ah, that's it, riiight there...!" Laviala's shoulders loosened, and she seemed to relax significantly.

I decided to mess around a bit and blew into those distinctive half-elven ears—not as pointy as elves', but definitely still pointy.

"Ffff."

"Ah, please stop... N-not my ears, not there..."

Laviala sank to the floor as her legs gave out under her. That was more effective than I'd imagined.

"Sorry. I didn't think that would happen..."

"D-don't do that sort of thing right now... W-w-wait until it's nighttime...," she said, blushing, which started to make me feel embarrassed, too.

"All right... Till nighttime..."

Having this sort of relationship with Laviala reminded me how quickly time went by. Up until a few years prior, we'd studied and practiced fighting with swords and bows together.

Just then, one of my vassals stopped by to say someone had arrived to meet with me. "The priest of the First Temple has come to pay his respects!"

The name First Temple referred to the temple designated by the local lord as the most important in their domain. Since there were many temples in a county, we had a ranking system for their regulation. Even now many of them (such as the biggest in a prefecture) had power like that of the nobility; however, at the county level, they all needed their lord's protection. Incidentally, this temple was the one where I'd received my profession.

"All right. Let him in."

The priest who came to pay his respects was the same one who'd granted me the Oda Nobunaga profession. He sported a thick white beard.

"It is good to see you again, my lord. I am the priest Elnarta. I never would have imagined you would rise all the way to viscount."

"Well, my brother fell ill, as you know. Nothing more than a twist of fate."

The official story was that my brother had died of illness, and I didn't plan to go out of my way to be known for fratricide. Chances were that he, too, would prefer that than for future generations to know he was killed trying to murder his brother, even if he only wished for it from the afterlife.

"Is the Oda Nobunaga profession serving you well? As the oracle, I had my concerns."

"There was no need to worry. In fact, I ought to thank you." I essentially had my profession to thank for becoming ruler.

"You are most welcome, Lord Alsrod. If I could have just a moment of your time, I would like to perform a phonetic evaluation of the words Oda Nobunaga."

A phonetic evaluation was a type of divination performed using the sounds a name made.

——Ha, what a joke. If divination truly worked, no one would ever lose a battle. All the warlords in my day had their own superstitions when they went into the fray.

My inner voice was complaining. He had a point, though. Generally in war, lords everywhere thought about luck when deciding which day or time to go to battle. If they could win by doing that, then nobody would ever lose. Certainly no one would ever give their child an obviously inauspicious name, either; by that logic, no one would ever be unhappy. But in reality, countless people had fallen in war or died young from disease. Nevertheless, I was genuinely curious what sort of result I'd get about this Oda Nobunaga.

"All right, see what you can do. It's not like it's going to take hours or anything."

"Yes, my lord."

The priest Elnarta spread out a cloth on the floor and sprinkled sand on top of it into the form of a magic square. He then wrote the name Oda Nobunaga in the center.

"I wonder what the result will be," Laviala said, also watching with great curiosity. She was always more interested in me than she was in herself.

"Oh my...," mumbled Elnarta. "Incredible..."

"What is it?" I asked. "Was the answer that unusual?"

"The sound that *Oda Nobunaga* makes essentially means the *Demon King*..."

"Demon King? The one who's supposed to lead monsters to world domination—*that* Demon King?" In this world, just as there were minority races like elves and dwarves, there were also evil beings like goblins and orcs. But a Demon King who commanded monsters was nothing more than a legend.

"Yes... In terms of a profession name like Fighter or Wizard, Demon King would be the most fitting name, I think... I apologize for any offense, Lord Alsrod..."

——Demon King, eh? A priest worth his salt, I see! Indeed, I did once call myself a Demon King just for fun!

My inner voice laughed. Without thinking, I laughed, too.

"Pardon me, my lord, but why are you laughing...?" the priest asked.

"Oh, no, it's just such good news."

Laviala seemed to understand how I felt. "A Demon King is still a king. You are aiming for the throne, not just Nayvil. This is the perfect profession for you!"

"Exactly. Of course, as king, I'll do my best to avoid being seen as a demon."

Oda Nobunaga really was a special profession after all. Laviala was spot-on: A Demon King was still a king. It was unheard of to receive a profession that included the word *king*. In a world with a more powerful dynasty, I might have been punished for irreverence.

"Um... No matter how much they have declined in recent years, the royal family still exists... Please try not to say anything too brash," Elnarta admonished me; perhaps he was just meek. Of course, if he'd tried to be agreeable by ensuring me I could be king, I would've lost trust in him. He probably didn't quite understand what kind of profession Oda Nobunaga was.

"Don't worry. If I get the chance to support the royal family, that's exactly what I'll do. But I'm still just a county-level ruler, so I'm a long way off from that." Claiming you were protecting a failing dynasty—only to go on taking power yourself—was an old trick for usurping a kingdom.

But then I had an idea.

"Say, Laviala, you still haven't received your profession, right?"

"I keep putting it off, yes... I just can't find the free time to do it."

It was true that Laviala, as my attendant, had trouble setting aside time, what with the sudden changes in my position.

"We have a priest right here. If it's all right to use the castle chapel, you should have your profession-bestowal ceremony there."

"If the chapel is in order, then the size makes no difference," Elnarta agreed. Of course it didn't; most peasants got their professions from a small village chapel, after all.

"All right. I hope it's something good..."

Thus, we made our way to the chapel. I wondered whether she'd also get some bizarre profession like Oda Nobunaga. Surely twice in a row was too much… And it would be especially awkward if hers was the name of one of his enemy lords.

The ceremony proceeded as it had for me. I call it a ceremony, but Laviala simply knelt while the priest relayed the words of the gods.

"Your profession is…Archer."

"Aw, that's more normal than I thought it would be," Laviala said candidly.

"Actually, Archer is a fairly rare profession…," Elnarta replied.

"It's far more normal than Oda Nobunaga," she replied.

I mean, I'm probably the only one in the world with that one.

Since Laviala had long made good use of her archery skills, it was a respectable profession for her.

"It is said that Archer raises your bow attack power by thirty percent in battle, and on top of that, it greatly raises your accuracy. Essentially, it will be impossible for you to miss your mark."

"I see. I'd love to try it out on a target right away."

Wanting to strike while the iron was hot, Laviala decided to shoot targets at an archery range we set up in the courtyard. Maybe it was my imagination, but I saw what looked like a golden aura from her body as she readied her bow.

"This is amazing. I'm perfectly calm, and yet I feel a sense of focus gently washing over me… I'm certain I've never felt this way before."

Then she fired an arrow.

Fwthoooom!

The sound was unlike any normal arrow I'd heard. Sure enough, it had struck the center of the target, leaving cracks and fissures where it hit. The power behind it would have been impossible for any normal arrow.

"Damn… Looks like one hit would be enough to kill a person…" Such power was more frightening than it was amazing.

"I don't fully understand it yet, either…," Laviala said.

"With Archer, it is said that if you have both the focus and the technique, sometimes magic from your body gets added to the arrow, and damage is tripled… This only happens with the best Archers, so I have never seen it before, either…" Even the priest was shaken.

Laviala was already a top-tier archer, and with the help of her profession, she was nearing divine status.

"I'll try it out a bit more." Laviala shot at a different target this time.

Fwbaaaaaam!

As soon as the arrow struck it, the target blew into smithereens.

"Whoa, it's as if you used an explosion spell on it!" I exclaimed. There was obviously more power in that strike than what an ordinary arrow could produce.

"I've never used attack magic, but I did get the same feeling as when I use healing spells... I suppose it did have magic..." Her shoulders were heaving a little as she breathed; maybe she'd strained herself. Still, her power was almost obscene.

Laviala had been trained with a bow and arrow from childhood, and since she had waited to receive her profession, she'd had to polish her skills enough to fight in battle without any such bonus. As a result, the sudden boost had made her that much stronger.

"Laviala, this is amazing! You'll be a terror on the battlefield now!"

"Yes, sir! I'll keep on fighting by your side and shoot any enemy we cross!"

Even with the priest there, I stroked Laviala's head. I might've found myself the best markswoman in the world.

"I'm glad I managed to get such an amazing profession."

"You're strong enough now to lead all the elves and half-elves in the domain; don't worry. You can hold your head high—or even be cocky."

We now had a helpful new fighting ability, too. While seeing to official business, I hadn't forgotten about territorial expansion. Now we should be able to crush the lords near us whose domains were close in size, one by one.

——Precisely. First you should take care of your enemies close to home, one at a time.

Oda Nobunaga agreed, so I couldn't be wrong. Whether Demon King or Conqueror King, I was going to be king.

"Laviala, practice your archery every day. You'll be using it for real before long."

"You mean...?"

"I plan to have the largest territory of any Viscount of Nayvil in history."

◇

I mustered my troops and advanced east. The Viscount of Nayvil (in other words, I, Alsrod Nayvil) held Nayvil County—home of the county capital, Nayvil—and half of the neighboring Hidge County.

The rest of Hidge County and Kinaseh County right next to it were held by the Viscount of Marle. Since his capital was in the rural Marle region, he'd taken that as his name. There had been tensions between our clans for generations, since neighboring lords generally got into territorial disputes. It would have been weird if we'd had long-term friendly relations.

So I was going to eliminate him first. It didn't matter what excuse I used to attack, but I said it was insulting he hadn't come to pay respects to the new ruler.

I went with four hundred troops. I could have gone with more, but this many was actually better. With these numbers, the surrounding lords would assume it was just a small skirmish between neighboring countries. (They weren't countries by name, but in this age, all domains were as independent as countries.)

Our troops clashed on a flat plain within the Marle region of Hidge County.

"Kivik and Laviala, I'm giving you each a hundred men. Go and crush our foes at once. This isn't enough to necessitate my involvement—yet."

"Yes, sir! Compared to the hellish days of Fort Nagraad, this'll be a piece of cake!"

"It'll be a bit lonesome not being by your side... But I'll destroy the enemy and come right back!"

They were both eager for a fight, and that eagerness saw results.

© Kaito Shibano

Just moments after the battle began, the enemy general was struck by an arrow that had seemingly come out of nowhere, sending his unit into disarray. It was only an arrow, but the damage looked more like the general's body had been pierced by a gigantic boulder—he died instantly.

It was clearly the work of Laviala, vastly powered up by her new Archer job. She could attack the enemy in places they thought were safe. She'd managed to hit their general with a shot that ought to have never found its mark.

The enemy soldiers trembled, perhaps thinking we had a rare Grand Wizard in our ranks, and they tried to run from our peasant conscripts. Soldiers without a commander were mere rabble. Kivik's company of veterans charged in, making it more of a hunt than a battle. Most of the enemy were prioritizing fleeing over fighting against us—it wasn't much of a fight.

"My bow is more accurate than ever!" With the enemy mostly vanquished, Laviala had returned.

"I knew it was you. I'll reward you later. In fact, I'll give you all the elf and half-elf units in the domain. I'll go ahead and grant you the rank of baroness, too. No one's gonna have a thing to say about it with the way you fight."

I'd been hoping to promote Laviala for a while now. I wanted her to join me in the upper echelons.

"Thank you, Lord Alsrod!"

"Thank me after the battle, when I've rewarded you. Now use your next shot on their clansmen."

"Yes, sir! I'll be happy to oblige!"

Giving out rewards here and there, we gathered our troops and captured all of Hidge County. Thinking this would be a little skirmish as always, the Viscount of Marle hadn't prepared the Hidge County forts' defenses against our attack. Thus, the enemy had no choice but to abandon Hidge County and withdraw to their home base in Kinaseh.

Overlooking the river in Kinaseh was a mercantile city called Maust. It'd be a mortal blow for the enemy to lose that area, so they took up position in the flatland ahead of it. They were clearly trying to stop our invasion in any way they could. The Viscount of Marle showed up, too; morale would have suffered if the ruler hadn't come.

At the moment, everything was going according to plan. Capturing the castle would require time, but if we fought on the flats, it'd all be settled in a day.

They'd taken formation so that their lord was set up on a low hill on the flats.

It really goes without saying, but the side with the high ground has an overwhelming advantage in battle. When fighting with bows or slings, too, the side firing downward gains velocity and therefore power.

Even in our war council, many were hesitant to call for an all-out assault on them, because of all the casualties it would cause. That was the natural reaction. But for some reason, I actually felt my heart pounding in excitement.

"They're not expecting us to come straight at them up the hill. That's exactly why they'll be off their guard."

——So you do have a knack for this. You know when an opportunity stares you in the face.

Oda Nobunaga was impressed.

——I struck down Imagawa Yoshimoto in a place not unlike this one. Back then, the enemy had likely let down their guard because of the rain, but here you have the power of your profession to make up for that.

He was talking about my job bonus. With the Oda Nobunaga profession, any foes within range of my weapon had their abilities reduced by twenty percent. Enemies cowered at the sight of a conqueror.

On top of that, the special ability Conqueror's Might doubled all my abilities during battle. Frankly, as long as there wasn't a master swordsman in front of their lord, it was impossible to stop me.

"I'll go in," I declared resolutely.

Several people cried out: "It's far too risky!" "Please, my lord, don't be so rash!"

That was precisely what I needed to hear from my vassals—I'd have been worried if they'd told me to just rush in there, no holds barred.

"Exactly—it *is* risky. And that's why the Viscount of Marle definitely doesn't think I'll come. None of them have the guts to face me. It doesn't matter how many there are if they don't have the will to fight. Their defense is riddled with holes, so much so that it'd be a waste not to attack."

The more I explained it, the more convinced I became that I could win.

"They have the terrain advantage. But that just means once we make it up the hill, it'll be a regular brawl, and then nobody will have the advantage. So listen: I need someone to use their shield to protect me as best they can until I get to the hill. After that, I'll eliminate their lord. Do I have any volunteers for my shield bearer?"

Laviala raised her hand right away.

"Laviala, I need you to cover me from afar. Your bow's of no use in close combat."

"Yes, sir…"

She looked unhappy, but those were the facts.

"Let me be your shield!"

A man raised his hand; he had come to be my officer back when I only had a village. Everyone here was the adventurous type, after all.

"All right, I'm counting on everyone's courage! We'll strike at night, when they can't coordinate an attack!"

To be honest, risks needed to be reasonably justified. There was more than enough justification for this war. If I could take out the Viscount of Marle, a neighboring lord with about the same amount of territory as I had, I'd be so famous I'd be hailed as a hero. I'd be far more famous than when I defended the fort with a small number of men. Strong warriors won't follow a commander whose strength they don't believe in, too. If

I demonstrated that I was the greatest lord in all of Fordoneria, my fame would last for generations to come.

That was why I absolutely needed to succeed—no, I *would* succeed. My goal was to become king. That was the best way to make not only me but also Laviala and my people happy.

This kingdom currently had many small clashes happening nearly every day, because the de facto independent lords were broken into countless factions. If I expanded my territory, squabbles wouldn't happen anymore in my part of the land. I was going to establish a peaceful nation.

And thus, night came.

I could feel it in the air—the enemy was at ease. The Viscount of Marle and his clan hadn't been in a real war in quite some time. And in a proper war, the side suffering a crushing defeat faced utter ruin, so unless they had a great deal of confidence in winning, people tended to avoid warfare altogether.

In particular there were a lot of small-to-medium-sized domains to the east of my territory. Almost none of the lords there controlled a prefecture as Mineria to the west did. That was why they all avoided full-blown warfare and only barely managed to protect their own land. Many lords followed a sort of unspoken agreement: "I won't attack you with my full force, so just look the other way."

Even with that going on, it was only a matter of time before the smaller domains were wiped out by a larger force like Mineria. Rules had meaning only when there was power to back them up. A single praying mantis trying to push rules onto a large cow still didn't stand a chance under its hoof.

"We start the plan now. I pray we can meet again smiling in the morning."

My unit made for the top of the hill where the enemy lord was. Of course, since the enemy had lookouts, they realized we were there and shot arrows our way, but our soldiers blocked them with their large shields.

We gradually drew near to them. When we were close, the enemy switched to swords and spears, trying to fend us off. Apparently, they decided they couldn't drive us away with arrows.

At last, the melee began and quickly turned to a bloodbath. Our foes had the terrain advantage, but they were as flustered as they were surprised at our attack. And they had us coming up the hill now, too. Now the side that felt like they were on the attack would be at a psychological advantage.

The area near me also became engulfed in the melee. I wasn't far from their lord now.

"Everyone, good job blocking their arrows! Now just worry about protecting yourselves!"

I leaped out from the shield wall and dived in, sword in hand. At close range, arrows were useless due to the risk of friendly fire. In a swordfight, though, I practically couldn't lose. One by one, I struck down each foe who tried to attack me.

Most of them still didn't seem to realize who I was. Since I'd drawn close to the enemy lord, I considered calling out my name. The effect on friendly morale would be greater. Besides, I needed to establish my heroism.

"Behold! My name is Alsrod Nayvil, Viscount of Nayvil! Bring forth the Viscount of Marle! Let's settle this with a duel!"

As the enemy soldiers, who had been wavering, realized I was there, their eyes lit up. Killing me would be a huge feat. Of course, I wasn't the least bit afraid; this had been my decision, after all.

I was as calm as ever, something the other side couldn't manage themselves. I just needed to close in on my goal, one foe at a time.

The more they went out of their way to attack me, the more their formation—protecting their leader—fell apart. It'd be a cinch to break through already.

Of course, there were other attackers on our side besides me pushing the enemy back. If we could reach the top of the hill, we'd be more than a match for them, since everyone on our side was fighting with all their heart.

I continued cleaving through all who stood between me and their lord. Against me, their abilities were automatically reduced, thanks to the He Who Seizes Power bonus. So unless they were far more skilled than I was expecting, there was no way they could win.

The vast majority who confronted me had looks of dread on their faces. It wasn't just a simple feeling of terror—more like they were witnessing someone of a completely different caliber from themselves.

"No, I'm nothing like any of you!"

My sword was nothing special, but that was hardly an issue. I cut up the enemies in front of me. I slashed, sliced, and hacked them down until there was a large hole in their defenses.

And finally, I skewered the final enemy before their lord. Visibility was good thanks to the moonlight, and my steps were nimble and quick. My breathing was more or less unchanged.

"Come, Viscount of Marle! Let us duel!"

My opponent was a middle-aged man of roughly forty years. He was stricken with fear at the mere sight of me.

"How...did you get all the way here...?"

——Just a pushover after all. Hardly the likes of a viscount such as yourself. No ambition whatsoever—he wouldn't know an opportunity if it struck him in the face. At least Imagawa Yoshimoto fought with everything he had, as far as I heard.

My inner voice was right. This man had no intention of fighting to begin with. He didn't even care to make a reputation for himself by killing me.

"Shit... I have to get out of—"

Unbelievably, he turned his back to me. My expectations were low, but not this low. At that point, he ought to have just abandoned the viscount title entirely. In my disbelief, it took me a second to start chasing after him.

Of course, it didn't matter. An arrow struck him in the foot, and he promptly fell over. The arrow was large, and it had pierced through all the way into the ground, with which he was now well acquainted.

"I am the Viscount of Nayvil's right hand, the eagle-eyed Laviala! This is what happens when I shoot cowards! Even in the dark of night, I never miss!"

I could hear Laviala's voice booming from afar. My ever-dependable milk sister.

I'll just take my time finishing the job.

"Sorry, but your time has ended—by my hand."

Slashing powerfully sideways with my sword, I cut off the enemy lord's head in a single stroke from behind. I immediately picked up his severed head—he must not have been much respected by his underlings, as none came to wrest it back.

"I have the Viscount of Marle's head! It is our victory—Nayvil's victory!"

The enemies who heard my cry broke ranks, fleeing in a panic. My men then charged from behind, slashing across their backs.

Just as I thought, they were so used to small skirmishes, they seemed to have no plan for when an enemy came at them in full force. By the look of things, I'd be able to put all similar opponents under my control, too.

——Ah, this brings back memories of my own heyday.

Oda Nobunaga was lost in thought over something. He, too, must've been unstoppable once upon a time, bringing his pathetic opposition to their knees.

——Although perhaps you could've used a little more backbone there, eh, Alsrod?

Well, we won, so I won't complain.

◇

With their patriarch fallen, the Marle clan fell into dysfunction and surrendered without so much as a show of resistance. For the time being, I decided to give their clan some land and incorporate them as vassals. If I killed off even those who admitted defeat, it would encourage other lords to resist until the end. That would only delay unifying the prefecture and otherwise accomplish nothing.

Thus, I was able to bring Hidge and Kinaseh Counties fully under my control. Altogether that made three counties I'd taken. With that, my goal of having the biggest territory in the history of the Nayvil clan had easily been realized. Still, that didn't mean there was nothing left to do.

I made sure news spread throughout the land that I'd single-handedly charged into enemy lines and taken the Viscount of Marle's head. There's no harm in making a name for yourself; besides, if warriors then came wanting to serve me, all the better. I would prefer to frighten the surrounding lords so thoroughly that they offered to submit to me, but even if they didn't, I would just wipe them out myself. Sometimes people only pretended to be loyal, so straightforward suppression by force was safer.

Upon my return to Nayvil Castle, once again there were an endless number of people wanting to come congratulate me. Painful though it was, there was no way out of it. I took time out to see people four times that day.

"No wonder my shoulders are so stiff lately...," I groaned.

"Well then, shall I massage them for you?" Laviala said playfully.

"Sure, just don't blow into my ears."

"Heeey, but you did that to me before! You're so selfish!"

Laviala toyed with me for a while, but we weren't on the battlefield anymore— having a little fun couldn't hurt.

The process of eliminating the small surrounding lords went on with near-frightening lack of difficulty. When there are many smaller authorities and one suddenly rises to powers, things become a one-sided fight. Now that I'd taken control of three counties for myself, the invasions and prefectural unification to come had instantly become easier.

First, I came up with some schemes to gather more enemy vassals to my side. Those who feared an attack from me generally joined without trouble. Then, when I attacked, these vassals would betray their rulers, and the enemy—already being fewer in number—would easily be destroyed. Even supposing they found out about it beforehand and purged their vassals, it would weaken their influence, which worked to my advantage.

Eventually, I gained control of seven out of twelve counties in Fordoneria Prefecture in the six months after defeating the Viscount of Marle. Since I had enough land by that point to reasonably call myself a count, I sent money to the embattled royal family, requesting approval to acquire the title formally.

Putting up these kinds of appearances was important, too. For example, for a viscount it was easy enough to submit to a demand of allegiance from a count, but if it was from another viscount, some lords couldn't agree out of pride. Lords in the countryside were essentially rural nobility. Rural or not, nobility was nobility, so there were many who worried about saving face. And that was why I needed to rise both in actual power and in form.

Without any fuss, the royal family gave me permission to use the title of count. Now I could take the name of the prefecture and call myself the Count of Fordoneria, but since I didn't control the entire prefecture, calling myself the Count of Nayvil would probably sit better with most. If I used the name of the prefecture, it'd provoke the rulers who still remained in power.

Once I became a count, I decided to spend some time improving my newly acquired territory. First, in places I wanted to develop economically around Nayvil, I created areas where it was free to set up shop. I spread to everywhere the same system I had used in my hometown market. I further changed the system so that people could open shops without joining the trade guild. Oda Nobunaga claimed this was called *rakuichi-rakuza*, which sounded like some sort of cultish incantation, but according to him, the *za* in this case referred to the trade guild.

I experienced some backlash from the trade guild, as expected, but I forcibly pushed the new system through as an order. When the trade guild had been established ages ago, it'd had value as something that protected merchants, but gradually it had turned into an organization that protected its vested interests. As a result, many trades became difficult for new merchants to enter. On top of that, the presence of the guild increased the prices of goods.

Because of my support of the markets, the cities developed quickly. I could easily tell the population of the county capital, Nayvil, was increasing, and tax income definitely was as well. Development of the cities was a plus for my country. (In the domain, laws set by the Nayvil clan were what mattered, so you could call it a country.)

Merchants from distant lands started to come, too. They must've had their eyes on us, realizing the kind of money they could make. Any money they spent here was good for me, too. As the cities flourished, I even decided to hire a financial officer.

"My lord, you look most well."

A dog-eared werewolf bowed his head before me. He was a wealthy merchant named Fanneria who'd apparently earned his wealth as an oil salesman and then branched out to do business in a variety of goods.

"Right. My territory has expanded, so I can't look after everything myself. I'm counting on you."

"Yes, my lord. It will be easier for me to do business, too, with your effective abolition of the trade guild. This era of small-time merchants in the guild must come to an end."

"I agree. That's why I hired you. Don't let me down."

"Yes, sir. I do believe that in all likelihood, there are places in the river-port towns that can be developed more. Please allow me to investigate. I suspect there will come a time when trade is conducted using large ships."

"Very well. Where circumstances permit, I'll fund renovation of the ports."

I needed to leave management of commerce to Fanneria for the time being, as I had to consider my relationship with the great power to the west—Mineria, ruled by the Count of Brantaar, where I'd fought with my life to protect Fort Nagraad.

The Count of Brantaar and his family, the Caltis clan, had controlled the entirety of Brantaar Prefecture for generations. The greatest city therein was Mineria, so the domain itself was called Mineria. The locals themselves used Mineria as their country's name.

We had a truce with Mineria for now. The agreement had been formally concluded shortly after I'd left the fort. I'd thus taken that opportunity to expand my power, so surely Mineria must've started to grow concerned by now.

And then, right on cue, they sent a messenger our way—not an actual vassal, however, but a priest. Using a priest as a messenger was common practice worldwide. We hadn't had a messenger from Mineria for a long time, so everyone in the castle was on edge.

Laviala in particular was glaring at the messenger as if to demand what the hell he was doing here. The messenger priest, however, seemed undaunted. Perhaps he was used to such treatment.

"I have come to offer our lord's congratulations on obtaining the rank of count," he told me.

"I see. I'm glad to hear that from one who has held the title longer than myself." Being instantly combative would put my rustic origins on display, so I'd decided to reply graciously.

"Currently, we are preparing to advance our troops north. As such, we would like to establish a stronger relationship with Nayvil than our current truce—an alliance. Would it be possible to hold a count-to-count conference just once? As for the location, perhaps a temple near the Mineria-Fordoneria border would be most appropriate?"

Interesting. Seems reasonable to hear out their proposal.

"Lord Alsrod, they could be plotting a surprise attack. Please be careful." Laviala immediately recommended I exercise caution. I was just as skeptical, myself.

On the other hand, the messenger had a smile plastered on his face. A crafty diplomat, indeed. At the very least, I couldn't imagine a man like this would be capable of leading people to heaven when they died.

"It is understandable that you have your doubts. I leave the decision to you. However—"

"Forming an alliance would free us from having to worry about our west flank, so this could be good for us, too," I interrupted. "If we were attacked by Mineria now, we wouldn't have the troops to spare for defeating other lords."

"I am glad you have seen the light."

That could've easily been construed as a threat to the effect of *Just try attacking us.* Mineria was still clearly more powerful than we were. They had about double the land area, a larger population, and a superior army to boot. Having controlled a prefecture for so long, they were likely more united than us, as well. In short, Mineria still didn't think much of me. They just saw me as a boy with ambitions who'd only just managed to claw his way to a title.

Apparently, Laviala had quickly realized this, too; a scowl had come over her face. "Did you come here solely to insult Nayvil and Lord Alsrod? You do know we could launch an attack at any time, yes?"

The messenger dismissed Laviala's retort nonchalantly. "If it came to war, I believe we could ally with Nayvil's neighbors and fight you together. I am sure you could not raise enough troops yourself to withstand an attack on all fronts."

Laviala looked furious. I was glad she had that attitude, though—and that the messenger had his.

"Very well. I will discuss all this with Lord Ayles Caltis of Mineria." I set the day and time for the conference and sent the messenger on his way home.

Laviala had much to say when we were alone together afterward.

"Lord Alsrod, why did you agree to such a thing? That man may have been polite on the surface, but he was really quite pompous! You are no less a count than his lord!"

"Like I said, it's fine. This way, if I can show him his impression of me was wrong at this meeting, the count will be ashamed to have looked down on us. Winning them over to our side is worth it. It's not yet time for conflict with Mineria."

"But how are you going to change the impression of someone who looks down on you?"

"I have my ways." I grinned. "First I'll train the hell out of the troops accompanying me. Not physically, but in discipline."

At this point, the vast majority of armies everywhere were just a hodgepodge of second-rate dawdlers. Most units really were a mishmash of peasants and the like. However, if those troops came with their steps all in sync, they would create a completely different image.

"They say that in the old days, the royal guard was beautifully disciplined; their steps even made a single sound together. I want to create a force like that."

"Can you do it in such a short time?"

"I'm confident I can. I'm not one to make excuses, you know."

Actually, I had gained a new special ability.

As a lord with the rank of count, you have gained the special ability Conqueror's Guidance.

The trust and focus of soldiers under your command is increased by fifty percent.

Using this special ability, I should be able to train troops even in a short time. Of course, relying only on special abilities would be a bad idea. Ultimately, profession bonuses were applied to your original ability. Someone without experience would only see a tiny effect no matter what bonus they had. In my case, if my men didn't get reasonably motivated to begin with, my hard-earned special ability would have hardly any bite at all.

"A massive army that moves uniformly on a single command…? Even knowing you as well as I do, that still sounds like a fairy tale…"

"Laviala, I never said anything about a massive army."

"Oh?" She cocked her head to the side like a little girl.

◇

What I was going to create was a smaller unit with only elite handpicked troops. No matter how powerful my Oda Nobunaga profession might be, there was a limit to what I could do with peasant troops who hadn't once undergone real training. After all, they were peasants, not soldiers.

Thus, I decided to organize a guard unit made of professional soldiers. If they specialized only in fighting, they should naturally be more disciplined. They could at least get plenty of time to train. While I was at it, I decided to make two units:

The Red Bears, with their arms and armor cloaked in red cloth.
The White Eagles, similarly adorned with white cloth.

This way, they could be recognized as something special even from afar, and those selected would be proud and motivated. I recruited volunteers from people I handpicked and who agreed to undergo intense training.

The men were rapidly assembled. Anybody would want to be someone special, especially these individuals.

——This is just like my Black Cloaks and Red Cloaks. Fascinating. I formed the Black Cloaks from my cavalry and the Red Cloaks from my pages.

Apparently, Oda Nobunaga had created similar units in his lifetime. But the Red Bears and White Eagles were still my original creation, of course.

——Now I get it. I figured out why I, a conqueror, was chosen as your profession.

And you want so badly for me to ask why, don't you? Well? What would that reason be?

——I believe that even in different worlds, there exist people with similar thoughts and ideas. You naturally have ideas that approximate Oda Nobunaga's. The things you've experienced aren't entirely the same, but some parts are very similar. That is why you were granted the Oda Nobunaga profession. Everything about this has been inevitable—not coincidental.

True—the history books clearly talked about people in completely different countries who had comparable beliefs. Of course, it's still strange that someone similar to me would become my profession. But professions are bestowed by the gods, so maybe that's not for humans to know.

——So you believe in the gods. Just take care not to get in so deep that it consumes you or makes you go soft. The gods are for you to use.

My inner voice seemed particularly verbose that day, but apparently, that was proof he was in a good mood. I had no complaints.

*   *   *

——In my youth, especially, I survived chaotic times by using several hundred elite troops. Fights between smaller groups of soldiers are decided by the men's training. A good plan is necessary for ten thousand to beat twenty thousand, but for three hundred to beat six hundred, you only need good men.

I found myself nodding unconsciously. With a thousand elite troops, taking a prefecture would hardly be a problem.

I assembled the Red Bears and White Eagles to carry out their actual training. Everyone put on the bands of cloth I provided, their expressions stern. Of course, they didn't look so severe out of criticism for me—these were faces full of determination. I'd made a name for myself not only at the battle of Fort Nagraad but also by taking the Viscount of Marle's head. Without a doubt, I had become the greatest hero among the neighboring prefectures, so no one here underestimated my abilities.

It felt good to have my combat ability in balance with my rank as count. Usually the higher up someone got, the less directly involved they were in battle. That much was only natural, as they couldn't always be on the front lines, but as time went on, they'd start to forget how their troops felt. That could lead to flawed decisions on the battlefield. In other words, the more aristocratic a person became, the harder it was for them to maintain a soldier's mindset. In my case, I'd become strong only after experiencing a great deal of misery on the battlefield. I had a perfect grasp of the suffering and despair of war.

"Listen up. I rose from being the second son of a minor lord up to my rank now as count by making a name for myself in battle. But you see, due to my sudden expansion of territory, my soldiers' training is no longer adequate for a count. This is a shame upon me, and it is a shame upon all of you."

I raised my voice to address the troops sitting before me.

"And so from today on, you will learn to move and behave in a manner befitting a count's guards. This is not for appearances alone.

Perfectly coordinated movements will strike fear into enemy lords, showing them our power is real. The training will be difficult, but I want you to weather it and come out stronger for it!"

""Hooraaaah!!!"" my men bellowed.

It was refreshing to hear. To think that so much had changed, compared to the time when the only soldier at my side was Laviala, was deeply moving.

But this still wasn't good enough. If I stopped here, so would my campaign.

In all likelihood, there'd come a time later when we'd have to fight against great powers controlling one or two prefectures. If we didn't get strong enough to win against such forces, then we'd be wiped out all the same.

"First is marching! Honor guards parading through the royal capital look stronger than soldiers plodding along; that should be obvious!"

I made them practice marching thoroughly, as I was sure that would be my most important weapon in the conference with Mineria. They were a large power, and military might always caught the eye of such people. Of course, you can't really tell how strong a military unit is by appearances alone. However, if you watch how its soldiers move, you can clearly ascertain whether their leader is competent.

What's more, I'd already given Mineria a taste of bitter defeat at Fort Nagraad. If I could make them realize that was more than luck on my part, the conference would definitely turn in my favor. They probably wanted to be relieved to see that this newly risen power was no threat. They wanted to think this youngster, not even in his twenties, was just a show-off. The messenger had made threats of combined attacks against us, but looking at it the other way around, that meant we, too, could team up with forces around Mineria.

They couldn't afford to ignore a power that had come to control more than half of a prefecture's counties in less than a year; that fact would trouble them. That was why they wanted to think I wasn't an enemy to fear. Suppressing us in the form of an alliance was even better.

Those must have been the sorts of things they were thinking. But

I wasn't going to give in to their expectations so easily. Instead, I was going to use Mineria to expand my own influence.

After two weeks of training, my guardsmen's movements made them seem like different people entirely. When I called "Ready!" they swiftly thrust their wall of spears forward. "Back!" returned the spears to upright. It was as if I were controlling magical puppets.

They were clearly bursting with motivation. It was easy to tell these men were far from ordinary troops. Of course, my special ability Conqueror's Guidance had an effect, but their natural motivation played a big part.

I showed the spectacle to Laviala, too.

"This is absolutely wonderful… I almost forgot to breathe…" She unconsciously held her hand to her mouth, clearly awestruck.

"I'm gonna show this to Mineria at our conference. I can't wait to see their faces—they won't know what to do."

◇

The day of the conference came. We held it across the river from Fort Nagraad, at a key temple in the area. No matter whose territory they were in, temples were ostensibly owned not by the respective lord but by the royal church—by the gods, even. Thus, they were often used for meetings. Of course, the lord's guesthouse was sometimes used, but since Mineria's central region was far away, there was nothing like that in the vicinity.

Because the conference was being held on their land, the rule was that they would show us hospitality, and their lord would be waiting to receive us. It was the perfect situation to show off my elite troops.

We took a break on our side of the river; I stayed in Fort Nagraad. That much went according to plan. Naturally there was no air of tension, as there had been during the siege.

"Pardon me, Lord Alsrod… If we don't leave soon, we may be late…"

Laviala came into my room in the fort, perhaps thinking it strange I hadn't given the order to depart.

"It's fine, Laviala; sit back and relax." I offered her a chair beside the table, and she took it.

"Forgive my asking, but might this be on purpose? Do you want to show your superiority by arriving late?" She was pretty sharp. But I had something else in mind.

"Even after we arrive late, the conference won't begin immediately. We'll then be removing our travel clothes, taking more time. Basically, they're going to have plenty of time to observe our troops. I'm gonna have them get a real good look at us."

"So that's why…"

"And since we'll be arriving late, I've got one more little show for them. You'll see when we get there."

And so we set out just under an hour behind schedule.

Naturally, we arrived at the conference location just under an hour late, too.

I'd heard from an agent I'd sent ahead that Ayles Caltis, lord of Mineria and Count of Brantaar, was watching my troops as they moved, so I made sure we went to the temple in a flawless procession. Today was the day. I could tell everyone was in high spirits.

——Mm, well done. The enemy lord will surely be frightened when he sees this.

The conqueror himself seemed happy as a lark, too.
They're not an enemy. It's not yet time to fight them.

——When I met with Saitou Dousan, lord of Mino Province, I deliberately brought second-rate troops and sullied my appearance, only to then surprise him by attending our meeting in formal attire. Dousan, having underestimated me, came dressed

informally and was floored to see me wearing such dignified attire. But making a display of grandeur in the beginning works, too. You're not wrong.

It was intimidation just the same, after all.

Thud, thud!

Mere steps, when in perfect unison, carried significant weight. I could tell the people of the temple and the Minerian vassals were dumbfounded as they watched us march.

"They're so orderly..." I could even catch what they likely didn't want me to hear.

My special ability Conqueror's Guidance made my men's trust and focus 50 percent greater. Even soldiers in service of the royal family couldn't march like this.

I arrived safely at the temple; however, I had another act to play.

"Good work, everyone." I turned about to face my men with a commanding expression. "However, there was an individual in the White Eagles who was not on time, resulting in our arrival being delayed. May the offender step forward." No such thing had happened. Naturally, I'd made it all up.

"Sir! It was my fault!" A young soldier fearlessly stepped forward. I stood in front of him...

Smack!

...and lightly slapped him across the face, my expression unchanged.

"Don't let this happen again. Be careful next time. If you're late to a battle, I may take your head."

"Yes, sir! Understood!"

"Back in line." He went back to his spot with a similarly stoic expression.

All of it was a complete fabrication. A commander who treated latecomers with fairness, a soldier who fearlessly reported his mistakes—I'd more than shown off my troops' discipline. I wasn't sure whether anyone was watching this little performance, though. Laviala looked as if she'd figured out the reason for the delay.

Now, time for this meeting.

When I entered the room, Ayles Caltis was already waiting. He was a man not yet forty, with fiery eyes. It'd be too much to call him a hero, but maybe the word *villain* would fit. Mineria had grown even more during his reign. He looked nothing like any of the hopeless minor lords I'd met until then. This man desired to expand his territory and make his land prosperous; I could see it in his face.

Behind me were Laviala and the veteran commander Kivik. Behind Ayles were two men who appeared to be part of his army's top brass.

"I sincerely apologize for the delay, Lord Brantaar. I misjudged my timing in these foreign lands." Before taking my seat, I gave the requisite apology. There was a special tension in the air unlike any I'd ever experienced. I'd never met anyone of this stature, after all.

——Yes, he's just like my father-in-law, Dousan, though far better-looking. To think they'd feel so similar!

Oda Nobunaga was carrying on about someone else, but I couldn't be so easygoing at the moment. I wasn't feeling on edge, however —in fact, I was rather comfortable.

"Please have a seat there, Lord Nayvil," he said. There were just enough empty chairs for everyone in front of the table.

"Don't mind if I do."

"Lord Nayvil, as we have only our advisers present, let us be frank. Hearing your troops would come late, I had the opportunity to watch them."

"Good gracious, we trained them so hastily—how embarrassing. You see, it's hardly been any time since I succeeded as head of the family, much less became count." My mouth was smiling, but my eyes weren't...probably. There were many gracious heroes in my time, but I wasn't one of them.

"On the contrary, if they were hastily trained, that would be far more disconcerting. Our defeat at Fort Nagraad was no fluke, I see. You're a tactical genius. In my honest opinion, I'd rather avoid fighting against you."

I decided to carefully figure out what Lord Caltis's true intentions were. At this point, I doubted he had a bad impression of me.

"Victory and defeat are all about luck. That I did not perish during the siege was mere coincidence," I replied. "Had I lost, I would be six feet under right now."

"Even so, it's rare to see a lord who can think on their feet like that. I still don't want to fight you—and you're not even twenty years old yet. At that age, you still have plenty of room to grow."

"I likewise don't want to fight with Mineria. That much we have in common."

"If you'd just been a pushover, I would've liked to get rid of you right away—but then you wouldn't have become a count in the first place, now would you?"

Laviala and Kivik suddenly looked as if they wanted to kill him.

"Do you have your assassins at the ready?"

"It would be difficult to kill you here. Even supposing I could, the moment I confronted you, I'd be killed myself. You're not a lord that's also a soldier; you're a soldier who became a lord. If we crossed swords, I wouldn't stand a chance. So firmly joining forces is best after all."

He really was an imperturbable man. And he seemed to admire my capabilities well enough.

"You don't have a wife yet, do you?" he asked.

"No. I've never had a chance to find one between battles."

"In that case, may I suggest you take my daughter as your wife?"

A political marriage to keep the peace with a threatening neighbor—a classic but worthy means. To be honest, I'd guessed he might say that, though I'd thought it would be once the conference had been going well.

"You believe an upstart such as myself to be good enough?"

"What's wrong with a count's wife being another count's daughter? It seems like a good proposal to me; what do you say?"

© Kaito Shibano

I glanced at my two vassals sitting on either side of me. Laviala looked a bit sad. She had been like my wife for quite some time, after all. I felt bad about it, too, but I was sure she understood.

Laviala gave a slight nod before confidently saying, "Lord Alsrod, by all means, you should get married. It's important now that both houses unite." She was my vassal to the end. If we'd both been commoners, I wouldn't have had to put her through this. She would've been able to ask me not to cheat, with confidence. I wanted to do something to repay her, even a little.

"Lord Brantaar, there's one thing I should mention in advance. Due to my position, I cannot be without children. I intend to cherish my wife, but I would like your leave to have concubines as well."

"Don't worry. I have several children by my mistresses, too. A lack of an heir can lead to civil war. Having children is another honorable way to protect your country."

Ayles was famous for having many lovers. Although in his case, many of them were daughters of lords he'd defeated. This was advantageous when assimilating the people of a conquered region, but on the other hand, there was a possibility those children would want revenge on Ayles for their clan, so it was risky, too.

"If I can have your daughter's consent, I will happily accept."

Ayles nodded deeply. "Very well. May I suggest you ask her directly, then?" He then loudly clapped his hands twice.

The doors in the back opened, and a young girl in a dress emerged. She was about fifteen or sixteen years old. Unlike her blond father, she had smooth jet-black hair. Maybe she was of eastern descent.

The determined expression on her face told me she was bursting to the brim with confidence. She was sweet yet not delicate—like a single sunflower blooming in a wasteland. I could feel myself getting lost in her large, round eyes.

"I am Seraphina Caltis, daughter of Ayles Caltis."

"It is an honor to meet you." I stood up to greet her. I had become a

© Kaito Shibano

count myself, but she had been born as the daughter of a count. I chose to act humble to satisfy her pride, to be safe.

She slowly walked up to me and grasped my hand tightly. "The honor is all mine. You're obviously a hero."

"I think you give me too much credit."

"It's been my dream to marry a hero. It would make life more interesting, don't you think?" She smiled from ear to ear, like a sunflower in full bloom. "I won't ask you to believe me, but back when you built that fort and created havoc in my country, I had a feeling I would marry you someday. I'd love to see you do it again—outside of Mineria. I'm sure I will enjoy the show."

"Indeed. If you'll be my wife, that would be my natural duty as husband."

"Yes, otherwise, I would have to either run away or kill you," she replied provocatively.

I could sense Laviala humphing, but to be honest, I thought I could get along with this girl for a long time—alive, of course.

"If you kill me, I think you'll regret it. I mean, there aren't many heroes to choose from."

"You really are a funny man, Alsrod Nayvil. By the way, my job is Saint. It's quite a rare profession. I'm told I can raise the luck of people near me by thirty percent. Fortune will surely turn in your favor." Luck was difficult to measure in percentages, but it was believable enough. Job-related abilities had been said to do as much ever since the olden days. "What's your profession?" she asked. "I told you mine, so you'll return the favor, won't you?"

"I think you'll be familiar with it. It's Hero, of course," I replied, gazing into her eyes. For just a moment, Seraphina blushed as if embarrassed. She may have been strong-willed, but she wasn't used to men. Besides, she was Ayles's daughter, of all people.

There was no such thing as Hero among typical professions. It was more of a concept than a job title. Even so, I really did intend to become a hero, and my Oda Nobunaga profession was more or less the same thing.

Seraphina turned to face her father. "Father, I'll be joining him in Nayvil. Thank you for raising me."

Ayles let out a sigh that seemed to include a great deal of different meanings. "You must have a sense of Seraphina's personality now, Lord Nayvil, but she's a smart girl. It's not parental bias when I say I think you'll be good together."

"Yes, sir. I'll do my best to make your daughter happy."

"For my part, I am happy for a man to rein in my daughter, though. I wish you both the best."

And so the conference between Nayvil and Mineria ended peacefully. The alliance was more or less established with the wedding planned. Both parties made a nonaggression pact and agreed that they would invade only unrelated territories going forward. Plans were made to make trade more convenient as well. For merchants with travel permits, protections were added, such as lending them horses to get to the other country and giving them priority at inns along the highway.

The formal wedding ceremony was set to be held a month later, at the same temple as the conference. It had been just a month since I'd first met Seraphina, and I couldn't help but say to her, "You look lovely." Seraphina was wearing her wedding dress; it looked so good on her, it was as if she'd been born to wear it. She was more vivacious than ever. "Tomboy or not, you really are a true count's daughter."

"I dressed up just for you, my dear husband!" Seraphina twirled around in front of me, and the fabric swished around her legs. "Make me the happiest girl in the country. My Saint abilities are even more effective on people I love."

"I guess you'll be making me even luckier, then."

Seraphina embraced me. "I really, truly love you, my darling!"

Back when I ruled half a village, I hadn't thought much of political marriages, but maybe this wouldn't be too bad.

As a wedding between count families, the ceremony happened in grand style. Priests and nuns from Mineria came and sang hymns to celebrate us. Of course, I was painfully aware this wasn't a bond of true love alone, but I still found myself tearing up. The ceremony was amazing. Even if our marriage never ceased to be political, Seraphina and I could surely be happy together for a long time.

"Honestly, my darling Alsrod! Heroes don't cry."

I'd been discovered.

"And neither do Saints, I'm sure," I shot back. Seraphina was crying far more than I was.

"But I'm so happy--I can't help it…"

If a historian years from now wrote that our marriage wasn't happy, because it was political, they'd be sorely mistaken.

Lords usually had concubines, especially powerful lords, but that privilege wasn't extended to noble ladies. A wedding really was a special thing for her, and I was a special man. There were a number of ladies in the kingdom, but unlike their male counterparts, divorcing and remarrying multiple times would only sour their reputation.

My soon-to-be father-in-law, Ayles, looked emotional to be seeing his daughter so happy. If you included the children of his mistresses, he had so many sons and daughters that he wasn't certain of the precise number. Still, it seemed he cared enough to cry for them.

After the ceremony was over, I took my new wife, Seraphina, to Nayvil Castle. She really was sharp; instead of anxiously peering around her unfamiliar new home, she immediately began criticizing its layout. "This castle is no good for a man of your rank. It's a bit too small. You couldn't even fit a thousand people in here! The moat around the castle town needs to be big enough for a count, too. It's not just a problem of family status; eventually your enemies are going to be bigger, too."

I stroked her head, even though vassals were present. "You're absolutely right. I was considering either adding on to the castle or relocating before long."

Nayvil wasn't a bad place to live. It was my hometown, so I felt some attachment to it. But it was ultimately the castle town of a minor lord governing a county. This far inland, it was hardly convenient; reaching the other areas I controlled took time. Even the castle had been designed to handle only a few hundred enemies. Against thousands, it could be overpowered with brute force.

"By the way, Seraphina, if we were to relocate, where would you want to go?"

"Well, I was thinking about your territory, and Maust is a good city since it's on a big river. It's convenient for trade, and with a good construction plan, you can use the river itself as a moat for the castle's rear."

I stroked her head again. "I'd have tried to marry you even if you were a commoner's daughter."

"So you like Maust, too?"

"Exactly."

Maust had been the commercial center for the late Viscount of Marle. I'd had my eye on it, too. In particular because Fordoneria Prefecture wasn't on the sea, meaning it was fastest to get to the ocean by going down the river.

"Once I can call myself Count of Fordoneria, I'll give relocation some serious consideration. First I want to take care of the other forces still in the prefecture."

"True. A hero can only show his strength in war, after all."

A vassal chose that moment to enter and said, with some reservation, "Sir, if you would, we have a number of documents that have yet to be taken care of..."

I'd been away from the castle for the wedding, so more work would be awaiting me than usual. There was no way I could personally show Seraphina around the castle and town now. Well, the size of my territory was nothing like before, so the amount of paperwork had risen exponentially, too. And there was a whole range of complaints I had to see to. And my official duties took forever.

"Very well. I'm getting back to work. Can someone show my wife around the castle?"

I'd rather it be a woman, though...

My eyes met with Laviala's.

...Not a good idea.

"I wouldn't mind... I can keep public and private matters separate...," Laviala had once said. I was happy she had, and I didn't think she would be unkind to Seraphina. But I was doubtful she was the right person, and there was a more fundamental problem.

"That half-elven girl Laviala is your lover, right? As such a master of the bow, she must have such a firm physique." Seraphina stared at Laviala provocatively.

So apparently, Seraphina considered Laviala her rival. I was acquainted with Seraphina's personality by now; she had a real competitive streak. Maybe it was all those siblings and half-siblings she had through her father.

"You're known for your valor, just like my husband. I hear you've felled many enemies with that bow."

"I am honored by your compliments, my lady."

"My chest is bigger than yours, though. It's at least twice the size."

Laviala blushed out of embarrassment. Her chest was undeniably small, a fact that probably bothered her, too. "If I may add, my lady...as I am an Archer, I am merely restraining my chest that it does not get in the way..." Laviala always made that excuse in public. I knew the truth all too well, but I used my better judgment and kept my mouth shut...

"So she says, but you know how big her chest is, don't you, my darling? What's the truth?"

"Don't ask me that!" I answered. I realized her intentions from her mischievous expression. She already knew the answer... Apparently, Seraphina really was a wild child.

"Ah, I understand. There are other vassals around, and I shouldn't embarrass your friend. You truly appreciate your position as count."

The other vassals present couldn't hold back their snickering. Even the elven vassals, who were close to Laviala, were laughing; it was obviously very common knowledge that Laviala was worried about her chest.

But I was impressed by something a bit different. With this exchange, Seraphina had instantly endeared herself to my vassals. Even as my wife, she was a daughter of Mineria, a sworn enemy we'd been fighting again and again. There may have been people who'd lost their parents in the war with them, and the political marriage was suggested by Mineria. Suspicion would be a natural reaction. However, with her banter, Seraphina had effortlessly eased tensions and earned herself recognition as the count's witty wife.

Seraphina glanced in my direction, as if to say, *What do you think? I managed that rather well, wouldn't you say?* My wife may have been more talented than I'd realized. And since some lords are too small-minded and incompetent to appreciate such a quick-witted girl, Ayles must have had trouble finding a good partner for her.

Meanwhile, Laviala was bright red. As far as she was concerned, she'd been sacrificed for Seraphina's reputation. "My lady... I wonder if you could perhaps not think of your position a bit more when choosing your words..."

"No need to be so formal. Call me by my name: Seraphina. I can't deny that you know my husband much better than I do, after all." Laviala's expression softened into something kinder. "You've helped my husband so many times; I know and admit that much. Please keep it up."

"Understood... Lady Seraphina..."

Rather than staying on top, Seraphina had let her opponent have the victory. She was good at winning people over. So good it was a bit scary.

"Well then, I hope we can be good friends, Miss Laviala." Seraphina suddenly extended her hand, which Laviala cautiously shook. I looked at Seraphina's smiling face and thought:

If I don't watch out, too, she could kill me in my sleep.

——Of course. A wild goose never laid a tame egg.

My profession said what I guessed was a proverb, like "The apple doesn't fall far from the tree" or something.

◇

Back to the question of who should show Seraphina around—someone other than Laviala would be better, after all. It was strange to ask your lover to give your wife a tour, though that was more of an excuse; in reality, I had too much work to do. Laviala was someone I trusted, so when I was busy, she was invariably busy, too.

But just then, the perfect person for the job arrived.

"I can show her around the castle, Brother," Altia sauntered into the room. She was much healthier than she used to be, and she'd even been well enough to attend our wedding. I could never have imagined such a recovery back when I was a puny, title-less lord with half a village.

Indeed, considering Seraphina had married into the Nayvil family, she and Altia were now relatives. There was nothing odd about Altia giving her a tour of the place.

"All right. If you would, then."

"Yes, Brother. I wanted to talk with Seraphina about some things anyway."

"Thanks, Miss Altia." Seraphina bowed her head politely. Since Altia didn't have a lot of friends anyway, it'd be nice if she and Seraphina got along. "Miss Altia, are there any saints of fertility enshrined around here?"

"Oh… Fertility…? There should be something…"

Hearing their exchange, some vassals laughed again. It was embarrassing to hear it said so plainly… I'd be in trouble if I didn't have kids, though…

"L-let's, um, recollect ourselves and get back to work…" Laviala was a bit rattled, too.

Pretty sure she meant "collect" ourselves. What are we supposed to recollect?

"Yeah, you're right," I agreed.

Laviala then said in a low voice so only I could hear, "I want to have your baby, too…"

"You will. No need to rush…" To be sure, a count needed an heir. But, well, there was only so much one could do. It really was down to luck, which was exactly why there were things like shrines to pray to.

I really did focus on my duties. Having reduced my pile of work, I held a war council in the evening to decide where to attack next. I invited not only Laviala and Kivik to attend, but my new wife, Seraphina, too.

Spreading a map out on the table, I declared, "We should attack Sanctum County to the south next. There's a group there called the Knights of the Sanctum who have another county. For them, captain is basically a hereditary position, so the current one holds the authority."

"Sanctum County… Ah, right, where the Fordoneria Cathedral is." Seraphina was correct. Since ancient times it'd been called Sanctum County for its cathedral, the greatest temple in all of Fordoneria. It had also been the political center of Fordoneria forever. In Nayvil there was the First Temple, which managed the rituals in the county, but this cathedral was where the rituals in the prefecture were managed.

"If we can take it, the unification of Fordoneria will be one step away. I'll bring them to their knees no matter what it takes."

"There will be absolutely no problem as far as how many troops we can muster. I'm sure of it," Laviala said confidently.

"In the experience of these old bones, there's nothing to fear, either," Kivik agreed.

——Exactly. Wipe them out posthaste. Anyone who fails to put even so much as a decent effort into diplomacy after your domain

has grown so much can't be strong to begin with. They can barely even grasp concept of fighting against large enemies.

Oda Nobunaga's words made sense. Whether it be joining forces with others or scheming to form an alliance with us, there were things they should be doing. They were a group who'd never even considered they might face great powers. For centuries, the pride of protecting the cathedral was the only thing that had sustained them.

"We're superior in both numbers and capability. However, there's one little thing bothering me." Everyone stared at me with worry, as if I'd said something ominous. "Ah, not that there's even the slightest chance we'd ever lose. I just need to be particular about the way we're going to win. I'm no wildfire or storm; I'm a count. I want to ensure something will be left after the fight."

"I'm sure we've been forbidding the men from pillaging. And I've kept a close watch on my elves," said Laviala.

"Ah, that's not what I mean. I have a plan. I'll take care of it on my own. With that, our total victory will be sealed."

After the war council, I consulted individually with someone else about strategy. The secrecy of this was important, so I did my best to hide it.

——I see, so you're going to use *rappas* as well.

My inner voice said something strange.
Rappas? What are they wrapping?

——No, no. The people you intend to use for this are called rappas. Good on you for lining some up. The more cards you have in hand, the better.

Can't argue with that.
Pushing through with brute force could cause a lot of problems. For the time being, I wanted to expand my forces more efficiently. I first

97

sent a letter to the Knights of the Sanctum, asking them to come pay their respects to me, the count. They were treated like nobility themselves, with the captain considered to be like a viscount. Thus, they were below a count. If they were to pledge fealty, they needed to come bow before me.

They weren't thinking of coming to do anything like that, though. The Knights of the Sanctum ignored the letter. As old-fashioned as they were, they didn't know how to deal with an upstart count. Besides, if they submitted to me, their vested interests in Fordoneria Cathedral might be taken away. They certainly couldn't allow that.

I advanced into Sanctum County with seven hundred troops. To be honest, it wasn't very many for a count, or someone with as much territory. I could've gone with double that. Some had insisted I use more men even if I risk my dignity. However, there was a reason I needed to deliberately stop at seven hundred.

One goal this time was to test the Red Bears and White Eagles. How impactful could well-led units be? I'd find out what differentiated them from regular soldiers.

And those elites and the units following them still barely numbered seven hundred at most. Oda Nobunaga had also said his elite units had numbered about seven or eight hundred when he had half a prefecture, so that meant I'd also brought about the right amount.

The results couldn't have been better.

A small battle played out on the flatland of Sanctum County, and the Red Bears and White Eagles—both with no more than fifty actual members—and their accompanying units of three hundred apiece mostly destroyed a force twice their size. The enemy was powerless against them.

We could have pursued them then, but overextending with a smaller force would have been a bad idea. Deciding to advance slowly, we made camp nearby for that day.

In the camp, Laviala, who kept ready beside me, listened gleefully to the battle report.

"They aren't even a bit coordinated. They fight in the old way, as chivalrous individual warriors, but their technique isn't even worthy of the descriptions."

"The Knights are actually a confederation of small independent lords, after all. It's impossible for them to move as one."

——Ah, like the rural warrior lords of Iga.

Oda Nobunaga was saying something to me—was Iga some kind of place name?

——The Iga lot were more of a pain than I'd imagined, but your foes don't have that kind of tenacity. They're just a collection of weaklings, more like the samurai lords of Yamashiro.

We'd had the upper hand in the first battle. I'd just keep up the attack.

I went on to batter the Knights of the Sanctum bit by bit. Having decided they couldn't take us head-on, they tried holing up in small hill forts, but we steadily destroyed their forts one by one.

Having made camp in a village, I called the captains of the Red Bears and White Eagles and showered them with praise.

The captain of the Red Bears was Orcus Bright. With his red face and red hair, he looked like a barbarian—a perfect match for the name Red Bears.

The captain of the White Eagles was an elven soldier named Leon Milcolaia. He had originally been a mercenary for almost thirty years and had come to serve me when I was lord of three villages. This man also had a fierce look in his eyes, like an eagle.

"Thanks to you, the battle is going very well. Stay on your guard and keep earning those medals."

"Sir! You are too kind! We will bring you victory no matter what!" Orcus replied. His sonorous voice made everything he said sound louder.

"We will fight to the end, so as not to sully the name of the White Eagles," added Leon, the more soft-spoken of the two captains.

"Ah, by the way, my lord, there's something I don't understand," Orcus inquired frankly.

Leon grimaced. *You watch your mouth around the count*, he seemed to be saying.

"Of course, Orcus. Go right ahead."

"Yessir. Why is financial officer Fanneria on the battlefield? I can't imagine a merchant would have much to do in a war camp."

True, Fanneria had indeed come along. His smile remained in place, even when his name was mentioned.

"Fanneria is a vassal, too. What's wrong with a vassal being here? Besides, there were plenty of merchants with their own troops in the past."

"Yessir, I am aware. But Fanneria isn't one of those bandit-type merchants, is he?"

"Do you have anything to say to that, Fanneria?"

Fanneria nodded. "Large-scale wars have always brought merchants with them. In a prolonged face-off, soldiers need to buy things, too. Merchants even arrange for prostitutes and entertainers —and that's why I'm here."

"Yes, I know that much. For that kind of work, I thought a lower-ranking merchant would be enough, not an official serving the count like you, but I don't mind your involvement, if that is what you want."

Orcus didn't seem to like Fanneria too well, but that was what happened when people had different positions. To tell the truth, Fanneria had a critical mission, but I couldn't really divulge that. If we could win without him having to fulfill it, that would be well enough.

But just then, a scout came in. "Reporting! There is movement from the Knights of the Sanctum!"

"Ha! We'll squash them no matter where they attack us!" Orcus declared theatrically. Leon again appeared to think Orcus was being improper. I'd purposely appointed captains with different personalities. Competing against each other here and there acted as an incentive.

"Well... They've barricaded themselves in...," the scout said despondently.

"Which fort? The Red Bears will crush 'em in one fell swoop!"

"...It's not a fort. It's the cathedral... Fordoneria Cathedral..."

Both Orcus and Leon were taken aback.

"I thought they might try such a tactic. I suppose they're no longer able to care about appearances." I sighed. I'd expected as much, but it was definitely still a headache. "They're daring us to burn Fordoneria Cathedral to the ground. If the cathedral gets damaged during the attack, people will wonder if we have what it takes to rule the prefecture."

"If they want to protect the cathedral, what're they doin' hidin' out in it?! They're more worried about themselves than they are about the cathedral! Petty scum!" Orcus was exactly right. If they really cared about the cathedral, they should fight out front. They were basically holding it hostage.

——Hmm, so this "Knights" lot can use their heads at times.

Oda Nobunaga actually seemed to be happy about their way of doing things. Enemies who schemed must have been more amusing for him.

——Personally, I'd rather burn them all alive, but it's a bit too early for you to rush into making a bad name for yourself. Lowering your reputation would delay your efforts to take over the country.

Don't worry, I've got a cleaner way of dealing with this.

"My lord, how should we go about this...? The White Eagles are prepared to break into the cathedral if need be... Our loyalty to you is more important than any faith..." Leon sounded like a true captain. My guard troops had already done more than enough, though. Going forward, I had something else in mind.

"Attacking right away wouldn't be so wise. For now, let's stall by issuing a call to surrender. I'd be mortified to be seen as a cathedral attacker."

I dismissed everyone there for the time being, then went on to call Fanneria to the residence where I was staying.

"I can see how the Knights have made it this long." According to the history books, the Knights of the Sanctum had used similar strategies to force enemy retreat about three times in the past. The most recent example was about a hundred years ago, so they didn't seem to want to use this method a lot, but they didn't have a choice now.

"Fighting for beliefs is all talk, of course. They're nothing more than lords themselves. They show their true colors when cornered," Fanneria said. For a merchant, he seemed familiar with the inner workings of the political world. He must've seen much of people's dark sides when he was still doing business.

"I want to put you-know-who to use. Are they ready?"

"Yes, of course. That's why I'm here, too. By the way…" Fanneria trailed off. The next part didn't seem important to me, either. "What shall we call them? It would be nice for them to have a name. I've just been calling them the shadowy ones."

I had a moment of inspiration. "Let's call them rappas."

"Rappas?"

"They're here to wrap up all the most difficult jobs and loose ends, wouldn't you say? They live to strike fear into the enemy." Oda Nobunaga was probably laughing just listening to me.

"All right, rappas it is. Rappas, come in."

In the blink of an eye, three werewolves had swiftly lined up next to Fanneria, prostrating themselves before me. This was my secret weapon.

"When a merchant becomes successful, more than a few attempts on his life are made. To put it in extreme terms, good merchants are those who get wealthy without getting killed, and bad merchants are the ones killed halfway there."

"So you hired special forces to protect yourself."

"No, technically it's the other way around. I was originally one of the shadow dwellers myself. When you spend so much time collecting information in secret, you start to know what places need what. It's a law of nature that you'll make money taking things to where they're needed. Besides, the older you get, the harder it becomes to serve as a frontline shadow."

"I see. That's true." It wasn't that uncommon for merchants to have some kind of military muscle; Fanneria was nothing unusual. Some employed mercenaries at all times as a de facto army. Otherwise, their property might get seized by some wicked lord. Still, there surely weren't many merchants who had a group of assassins steeped in backdoor work, like Fanneria did.

—Huh, so this world has its own sort of *shinobi*. The human mind works in the same ways no matter where it may be.

My inner voice's world was no different, apparently. It was harder to imagine a world without assassins.

"Listen. The Knights' leadership is holed up inside the cathedral. I want each of you to kill two or more of them. Then they'll be down at least six. If they lose that many, they'll be entirely unable to function."

The Knights of the Sanctum, by principle, decided matters with a knights' council. Their captain had authority, but not so much that he could order around everyone as he liked. There were about twenty member knights; their respective clans made up the rest. Thus, if six of them disappeared, the rest should give up. Most likely, they'd be too scared to even consider defending the cathedral.

"And when should it be done?" Fanneria replied. The rappas didn't speak a word.

"I'd like to say right away, but let's try bargaining a little longer. If we can divorce them from the cathedral by talks, that works, too." For my part, I just wanted the Knights of the Sanctum gone, so there was no meaning in taking away the cathedral's assets. The cathedral itself had no military, so its people couldn't openly defy me.

The next day, I sent them a letter with the following message:

- *I ask that any fighting take place outside of the cathedral, as it would be unsavory to sully the cathedral by hiding within its walls.*
- *As count, I will contribute necessary funds for the operation and preservation of Fordoneria Cathedral.*
- *You will be subject to divine punishment for the blasphemous act of attempting to wage war in the cathedral.*
- *Any knights who surrender will be treated with leniency.*

We received no particular response. My goal was to repeatedly let them know that I had no intention to harm the cathedral and that I wanted good relations with its people. Sanctum County was practically already established as my territory, so I wanted an amiable relationship with them.

Thus, the deadlock went on about another week.

During that time, I received news about the goings-on inside the cathedral. As I'd thought, seven of the Knights' most influential members were inside the cathedral, and the rest were commanding troops, keeping watch around it.

It's time.

I gave Fanneria the order. "Do it."

"Yes, my lord." Fanneria nodded, and before I knew it, three wolves were lined up next to him. "We've already ascertained the enemy's positions."

"All right, I'll expect a good report." Part of me still didn't fully believe it would go well, but as it turned out, the swift results were even more incredible than I'd imagined.

Around dawn, I had visitors at my quarters; I got up right away. The three rappas were lined up, and Fanneria was with them.

"Seven knights are dead, including the captain. It seems the cathedral was stained with blood somewhat, but that much can be forgiven."

"How anticlimactic. Is infiltration such a simple thing to do?"

"This sort of thing is impossible without being sure of success. We only made a move because I judged there to be no way the rappas could fail with their skill. Actually, you could say prior investigation is eighty percent of a rappa's job."

Since the rappas did not speak, Fanneria had much to say. A merchant has to talk himself up to make sales, after all; no merchant believes in action without words.

Now there was no way the remaining knights would band together to fight. They'd fear being the next target. Some of them would offer to surrender, so it'd be impossible for them to band together.

"Good work. I'll send another letter in the morning. I'm sure their reaction will be different from last time."

There was a stir well before that, however; priests and other associates came to me looking for protection. The head priest said they'd been all but completely detained by the Knights, so when they realized most of them were dead, they just ran out without looking back. The Knights of the Sanctum could no longer justify their existence. They couldn't even say they were defending the cathedral anymore.

In the end, some of the remaining knights fled, and those who stayed till the end gave themselves up. Due to their defiance of my call to surrender, as well as their disrespectful treatment of the priests, I stripped them of all their territory and gave some to the cathedral. Thus, Sanctum County, as well as the other county the Knights had held, came under my control. Nine of the twelve counties in Fordoneria Prefecture were now in my domain, and control of the entire prefecture was in sight.

Furthermore, I cited the official reason for the Knights' deaths as "divine punishment resulting in their mysterious demise." With the Knights being eliminated, nobody came out to object anyway. Naturally there were people who weren't satisfied with that explanation, however.

I returned to Sanctum County for a few days to oversee my new territory. One night, when Laviala and I were alone, she asked me, "Lord Alsrod, when did you hire assassins?"

Guess she knows it wasn't divine intervention.

"Oh, a little while ago—and by that I mean I can't afford to let the public ever find out."

"You're not even going to tell me?" She sounded so sad; it kind of made me want to tell her, but…

"You just want to know everything about me, don't you? But you're my vassal, and that's not your decision to make."

"Oh, that's true…"

Leave your feelings out of this, then.

"This is to make up for not telling you." I drew her body close as I kissed her.

◇

Yet another benefit came from capturing the cathedral with cunning rather than with force. I was invited into the cathedral by the head priest the day before I was set to leave Sanctum County. I entered the cathedral, taking just a few attendants, including the two captains of the guard. Even if there were assassins present, I had more than enough vassals at my side to fight them off. The people of the temple, including the head priest, assembled to meet me.

"You have our utmost gratitude for saving us from the temple knights the other day. And we cannot thank you enough for enduring patiently to the end and choosing not to attack the temple itself."

The head priest was a man named Tenny. Apparently, he was the third son of a high-ranking official from nearby the royal capital. Tenny had entered the priesthood at a young age and worked at temples all over for more than fifty years before coming to serve as head priest of Fordoneria Cathedral after turning sixty.

"No, I just did what a count ought to do. I've been using the title

Count of Nayvil, but I've always dreamed of all of Fordoneria being at peace."

"Your energy has already reached the farthest corners of the prefecture. There is nothing stopping you from taking the title of Count of Fordoneria." Tenny's response did reek a bit of bootlicking, but it was true my forces were almost big enough to go after the whole prefecture.

All that was left were the three counties in the northeast part of the prefecture. Those three were divided up among eight small lords.

"I'll think about taking the title Count of Fordoneria after I get back to my castle; I still don't control the entire prefecture, after all. So what was it you called me here for?"

"Your military prowess is well known, even to us servants of the gods. I thought maybe we could give you something to go along with your bravery." The head priest signaled to an aide with his gaze, and the aide immediately brought over a long, narrow wooden box.

"What could this be?"

"Please open it. It is our present to you, my lord."

When I opened it, there was a single extremely long spear inside. The spear was shining so brilliantly, the light seemed to be coming from the metal itself. I could tell just by looking at it that this was a very finely made weapon. It was common for influential families to make an offering of a weapon, to represent the defeat of evil or victory in battle. It wasn't strange at all for the cathedral to have a weapon of the highest quality. Still, this had been made for a god to hold, so it was too long for a normal person to wield.

"For me to take something that was offered to the gods..."

"You need not worry about that; by all means, try holding it. A count needs a symbol of power worthy of himself."

Reckoning maybe it did suit me, I took the spear as suggested. It felt perfect in my hand and strangely familiar somehow.

——Ah! Now this here is a weapon made for a conqueror! It makes one want to start a war just to try it out!

*   *   *

You know about weapons, too, Oda Nobunaga?

——No warrior doesn't find them fascinating. Still, when it came to collecting, I preferred tea utensils—they're more interesting.

Tea utensils? Not exactly a hobby for a conqueror.

——I beg to differ. Actually, tea might be the best symbol of peace. No king is coronated wearing armor. A conqueror has to cast his weapons away sometimes, you know. If you do nothing but fight, then you're not a conqueror yet.

I knew what he meant, but it was a bit sad, too. Fighting was fun in its own right. But enough of that; Oda Nobunaga had said something that intrigued me.

You consider this a weapon?

——What a strange question. This is clearly a spear.

No way—this thing's too long.

——Have this world's prejudices gone to your head? The longer, the better, as far as I'm concerned.

With that, I finally understood the spear's true value. Oda Nobunaga was right—I'd let my own silly prejudices get in the way. Best to get rid of those sorts of things.

"May I accept this, truly?"

"Yes. Actually, if the knights in the cathedral hadn't died when they did, they might have run off with precious weapons like this. We're just not able to protect the cathedral's things. If that's the case, I would rather we presented it to you, the Count of Fordoneria."

"I happily accept." I respectfully gave thanks. This spear was more than just a keepsake, for it wasn't the spear that was valuable; it was the idea it gave me.

◇

I made my triumphant return to Nayvil Castle. I'd expected a warm, happy welcome from Seraphina when I returned, but she was actually in tears.

"Honestly, darling! Don't leave me all alone for so long… I was so, so lonely, I didn't know what to do!"

Running into my arms, Seraphina pounded lightly on my chest. She wasn't angry; she really was as lonely as she had said. It almost felt as if I had another little sister instead of a wife.

Seeing the count and his wife so in love, the people nearby looked on warmly. Being unemotional was perfect for war, but in front of my wife, even I wanted to be kind.

"War is my job. What do you want me to do?"

"But…you took your soldier girl Laviala with you… I'm sure you had lots of fun together…"

This seemed like trouble. I looked over at Laviala, and sure enough, she'd turned red.

"That… Well, once the war cooled down, just a bit…," I admitted.

"I knew it. I'm your actual wife, you know, darling."

My sister Altria showed up just then, looking a bit annoyed. "While you were gone, Seraphina was praying for your safety, you know. You should be more appreciative of her."

"Right, fair enough…" My sister and my wife seemed to have bonded considerably. They were close in age, after all.

A few days later, with the spear I'd gotten from the cathedral in hand, I stood in front of all my vassals.

"Up to now, I have called myself the Count of Nayvil. However, the head priest suggested I assume the name of the prefecture. Therefore, from this day forth, I shall take my place as Count of Fordoneria."

*　　*　　*

Not a person objected. I nodded my head magnanimously. "And so I'd like to perform my first duty as Count of Fordoneria."

Some of them shouted, "At last, it's time to unify the prefecture!" To make a long story short, no. I could do that later.

"I'm going to move my castle from Nayvil to the river-port town of Maust."

"I'm going to move my castle from Nayvil to the river-port town of Maust," I declared unequivocally.

Some of my vassals were bewildered, though I'd expected as much. Their faces betrayed them. Leaving a place you'd grown used to was hard; it was a natural thing for anyone to feel. However, I had something else to prioritize over such feelings.

"Nayvil Castle was only ever a base of operations from when I was lord of a county and a half. This place is too small for our endeavors to come—it's not even on the main road. We're therefore moving to Maust, in Kinaseh County. There we'll build a castle more than twice the size of the one now."

As I'd already told some of my senior vassals about the move, they showed no sign of surprise. Seraphina wasn't present, but when I talked to her in the bedroom, she was delighted, saying, "You made the right choice!"

"Might...it possibly be a better idea to move your capital after you've unified the entire prefecture...? With the prefecture stabilized, it ought to be easier to gather the materials...," said an older vassal, who'd actually served in four administrations since the time of my grandfather. I was happy for his loyalty, but unfortunately I didn't think he had much foresight. It wasn't his fault. His manner of service was outdated.

"We'll have to leave here eventually either way. Besides, moving to Maust soon will help us fund our campaigns, too. It's a river-port town, after all; going downstream can even get you to the sea."

"In that case, Nayvil has plenty of crops and is flourishing, is it not? Even I can't quite recall a time when money was a problem."

Oda Nobunaga was the first to laugh—though all his laughter was almost annoying.

——This old man doesn't even understand the most obvious things. There's a world of difference between the money you get from having a commercial center and the money you get from farming. As a city already famous for commerce, this Maust place would obviously earn you more money if you developed it as your capital.

Exactly. One or two hundred years from now, there wouldn't be any lords living like they do now. Bit by bit, smaller lords were being absorbed by larger powers. Even Mineria, in the last twenty years or so, had essentially consolidated power by eliminating disobedient vassals. They'd slowly made it possible for themselves to expand outward.

Of course, people like this old vassal, who still thought in the old ways, would be gone before long. Also, I wanted to move my capital to Maust because I was thinking beyond the prefecture's unification. Going downstream, you could reach Nagurry Prefecture to the north. It was the perfect direction to attack from as we kept the peace with Mineria, and there were several seaport towns in Nagurry.

In a large-scale war, most soldiers had to be conscripted from the common folk, but as my guardsmen had demonstrated last time, professional soldiers were much stronger militarily. And it would take money to expand my guard units while maintaining their quality. Going forward, I'd need a system to collect more money if I were to go on becoming a great power. A port town where trade could be conducted would be more convenient for that. Moving the castle might also help me filter my vassals somewhat.

"You're right—relocating would be a burden on an old man like you. So you can stay in Nayvil."

"No... That's not what I meant..."

It was probably better not to let naysayers come along. If they had an even better idea to propose than mine, that'd be great, but most of them just wanted to say no.

"Nayvil is the birthplace of my clan. Don't worry; this land will always be an important place for the Nayvils. It needs someone to look after it. Please, I want you to stay and serve my family and my ancestors who were laid here to rest."

"Actually, compared to Maust, I think this place is more—"

Wham!

I struck the floor with my spear. The room fell silent.

"Have you even once considered there might be a better spot than Nayvil in this prefecture?"

"N-no, never…"

"Well, then have you ever gone around and visited the castles of lords who control a prefecture?" I glared at the old vassal. At first I'd just meant to put on a show, but as I glared at him, I started to actually get angry.

"Never…"

"In other words, you were just saying no without a reason. That's not advice or anything else. Maybe wait to open your mouth until you have something to say."

"Forgive me…" He bowed down before me, all the way to the floor.

Laviala nodded as if to say, *Good*. I'd told her about my plans in detail. She was a great listener.

——No matter where you are, there are always dissenters when you try something new.

So Oda Nobunaga had to deal with that, too, huh?

Though obviously a man calling himself a conqueror wasn't going to be conservative.

——Tradition definitely has its place. I took full advantage of it when I could, myself. I was always very careful about my reputation. But tradition is also a tool, not something to follow thoughtlessly.

*　　*　　*

Good point. You know, your ideas are always pretty helpful.

The greatest perk from the Oda Nobunaga profession might've been the advice I got. If Oda Nobunaga was famed as a conqueror in another world, I was hearing that conqueror's direct opinions. Without a doubt, it was more valuable than any counsel I could hear from the wise men of this world.

"All of you, your apprehension is to be expected. None of you have ever served a lord with this much land, after all. Your way of thinking will change in time. What I'm trying to do isn't anything outlandish. My goals are realistic."

Putting them in their place wouldn't do any good if it made me too intimidating, so I gave them a smile. "Don't worry so much. We couldn't move in just a day or two anyway. But start getting yourselves familiar with Maust's landscape at least. I would also like to share one more thing I'm considering."

I struck the floor with my spear again. Not with as much force as before, though—I wasn't trying to scare anyone. "This spear I received from the cathedral is long indeed. It's over three jargs." One jarg was about equal to the height of a tall man—most people were shorter than one jarg. In other words, this spear boasted a length greater than three large men.

"It's certainly imposing, but it was an offering to the gods, after all. It's too long for a weapon," said one of my vassals.

"You'd think so, wouldn't you?" I chuckled. "And that is why I'm going to put it into production. I'm going to assemble a unit that can use this. They shall be called the Tri-Jargs."

A few vassals laughed, seeming to think it was a joke. There were neither military units nor tactics that used a three-jarg spear; it was only ever meant to be used by the gods. Nothing this long was meant for humans.

"You have a great sense of humor, my lord. Can we call you the lord of the century, already?"

"Forgive me if I was unclear, but that was no joke. Of course, I don't mean to say anyone could use this very easily. Orcus, try giving it a swing." Orcus Bright, captain of the Red Bears, stepped forward as called. Few men were so obviously a soldier as he, with his log-like legs and arms.

"I can give anything a whirl, even a weapon this long!" Orcus swung the spear up and down, again and again. His body trembled just a bit, but it seemed he could do it. He yelled "Hwah!" every time he swung the weapon. The great length made it so much more impressive. It was entertaining in a different way from martial arts demonstrations.

"It's definitely hard to keep posture when it's twice as long as other spears! I can't swing it in a circle... Ah, how embarrassing..."

"If you can already do that much, I think you can make it work with some practice."

"Certainly! I'll give the Red Bears thorough training, too; we couldn't call them the Tri-Jargs if only I could use it, after all. Besides, a spear corps isn't any good with only a few members." He really was a soldier to the core. That made things easier.

Swinging spears down all at the same time in a tight formation is what makes a spear corps a threat. The enemy can thus be worn down by the spears before they can even get close. If their defenses seem weak, everyone can move in together to stab them, as well.

"If a unit could make a tight formation using spears this long," I said, "they'd be terrifying both offensively and defensively, don't you think? Not even cavalry could break through it. Smashing the horses' skulls would be a cinch. And of course, we'd be at an advantage against other spears."

"Indeed! They'd tremble at the mere sight of us! I shall master this monstrosity of a spear no matter what!"

I'd had an idea when I got the spear from the head priest: What if a human could use this weapon meant for the gods? There was, of course, a limit to the human body. A fifty-jarg spear couldn't even be held up, much less forged by a blacksmith. A three-jarg spear, though, could be wielded once you got used to it. And it should put on a great show of power.

Spears were meant to be used in tight formation anyway; they weren't for someone to run out and use on their own. So we could teach them to use even this three-jarg spear at a basic level of competence.

A vassal raised his hand then, looking uncertain. "My people aren't very strong, so I don't have confidence they could tame such a spear…"

"I'm aware of that."

"But aren't you going to have these three-jarg spears used everywhere?"

"First I'm going to try having professional soldiers use them—my guardsmen. I've no intention of making all the peasant conscripts use them, so relax."

This spear was heavy, so only men strong enough to endure tough training would be able to coordinate with one another. A group of spearmen that moved out of sync was just begging the enemy to break their way in.

"If even peasants could use it, another lord somewhere else would've done the same thing ages ago. So people making their living off war should be the first ones to use it."

——Alsrod, you really do think like I do! How amusing, how very amusing! This is just like the spear tactics I used—and those spears were twenty feet long!

Well, isn't that a coincidence? But everyone knows longer weapons are advantageous in battle. Some things in war are universal.

——Exactly. That's why it's so much fun for me to see you coming up with the right answers!

If he was telling me I had the right answer, the Tri-Jargs should be worth it.

◇

In the middle of the Tri-Jargs' new training, I turned twenty years old. It was nice to spend my birthday as a count. That day I put aside work, and Altia, Laviala, and Seraphina held a celebration for me.

My work wouldn't involve weapons for a while. I wrote very polite letters to the independent powers still left in northern Fordoneria. To summarize, they went like this: "I've been busy putting down scoundrels and blasphemers, but I'm finished with them now. Let's keep things peaceful." Obviously, those were only words. Any lord who took diplomatic platitudes at face value should just go be a priest or something.

Still, it would be risky to outwardly provoke the remaining powers. Even if they were each weak on their own, they would be trouble if they asked for help from the Rentrant clan of Nagurry Prefecture to the north. The Rentrants were a line of counts who had controlled Nagurry for generations. They didn't seem to be that strong at war, but Nagurry had several port cities with a large population. They could muster more troops than we could. It might be exaggerated, but there was a story of them raising over five thousand troops for a single battle in the past. Five thousand in one place would be unprecedented. They must've gathered troops from port towns that had their own mercenaries.

At the moment, the most troops I could raise at once would be a bit under three thousand. Of course, there was no need to fight a total war, so I'd never raised that many. A few hundred men had been enough to defeat my enemies. Even if I did manage to unify my prefecture, the number I could raise may or may not reach four thousand. In practice, I'd have to distribute them into different task forces.

Of course, I had something else to do before calculating troop numbers.

I went to Maust and checked the plans for the castle. It was going to be the greatest building our prefecture had ever seen, after all. I couldn't guarantee it'd be completed properly if I didn't at least go give instructions directly at the site.

"See, first you need to make the castle's south and east sides face the winding river. If anything, draw the river in around the castle so it looks like it's floating."

The people I'd brought in for the design seemed to be in disbelief. "A castle that appears to be floating…? It certainly would be defensible, but according to these plans, it seems it won't be connected to

117

the castle town…," said Ornis—basically the construction foreman of this project—a bit confused. He had originally been a salt merchant in Maust. I was now much more powerful than I had been as a little viscount, so vassals who had served my clan for generations often couldn't keep up. I'd appointed merchants and former vassals of other clans for a variety of things.

"No, this'll work," I said. "We'll build a waterway to the preexisting town of Maust at the same time. That will provide a direct route to the castle. Of course, it wouldn't work for only ships to get through, so we'll also build a bridge to link the castle towns to each other."

"This is going to be a huge project…"

"How long will it take?"

"It'll probably need three years…"

"Do it within one." Ornis was speechless. Well, apparently people couldn't help but balk at a large project they'd never done before. "Fine. I'll help give instructions, then."

"Y-you're going to help?"

"The castle is like my home. What's wrong with coming to the work site for your own home?" Encouraging the construction psychologically was part of it, but I also had my profession's assistance in mind: the special ability Conqueror's Guidance. If the laborers' focus and trust were 1.5 times as great, it should be possible to make things take shape quickly.

"I shall do what I must as well… However, the cost for this castle will be tremendous…"

"My financial officer, Fanneria, says it's possible. From here on, more and more people will be coming to Maust, too. What's Maust's population now?"

"About twelve hundred."

"Once it's the prefectural capital, I plan to make it about six thousand."

"Five times its current size?!" He was overly astonished at every little thing.

"I know it's unprecedented. But that's how big we need to make it. This might come to be the center of the world someday, you know." I wasn't sure he took my word at face value, but I was serious.

*　　*　　*

The construction of Maust Castle proceeded smoothly for such a large engineering project. Of course, it wasn't just about building the castle. The town would also be revamped alongside it.

As for the economy, I suspended the trade guild and allowed anyone to set up shop at the market. I mostly changed the system to the one I used back in my three villages and Nayvil, where tax was taken only from those with a profit.

If there was a guild, people would have to join (and pay inspection and enrollment fees, of course) in order to have a shop.

On top of that, since prices were controlled internally, things that would normally go for less would be more expensive. This was good for protecting the traders, and the lord could also take money from the guild, in the end. Of course, the Nayvil clan themselves used to protect the trade guild in the county capital, Nayvil. It wasn't a bad way to do things when they wanted to keep the town as it was.

——Apparently, people thought I made everything into a _rakuichi-rakuza_ free market, but I protected the _za_—the guilds— when I needed to. I didn't completely abolish the _za_ or anything like that.

Even my own job said as much. _Za_ was a weird-sounding word, though. It was almost too short to say.

Anyway, guilds were useful only as long as a city didn't get much bigger. I had proclaimed before that I was going to make Maust the prefectural capital, so the population spiked. That would mean more people would want to do business, so there needed to be more shops and markets. I had no need for a guild to hinder progress in a city like that.

There was pushback from the guild, but I brushed it aside.

"I'm more or less an invader in Maust. I'm not going to follow in the footsteps of the previous lord," I explained. "Besides, the lot who did business here originally can turn their experience into profit. Realize you're saving money by not having to pay the guild. You will have to pay me tax out of your profits, though."

The guild didn't even have the power to resist. They backed off in dejection.

Besides, trying to tax the poor wouldn't get you anywhere; there was only so much they could give. In that case, it was better to let them make money and then to take more from that. Oda Nobunaga himself said he made tons of money by controlling a port town called Tsushima, as well as another city called Atsuta. It was definitely best to have an economic foundation to support military endeavors.

Taking Maust was huge; compared to the cities I'd had before, the amount of taxes I got was literally an order of magnitude greater. With my swelling pocketbook, I hired more workers. Where we needed more help, I levied the peasants to some extent, but I paid higher wages than in the past. The more workers there were, the more people came to sell them things. It made for a good cycle.

Eventually, I received yet another ability.

Special ability Conqueror's Insight acquired.
Your economic sense related to cities and trade will be akin to Oda Nobunaga's. This ability is constantly active, barring intoxication or any impairment to your mental state.

The heck...? Is this actually an ability...?

——Allow me to explain.

Oda Nobunaga spoke to me again.

——As you said, this isn't so much an ability as a show of my admiration. I'm recognizing your foresight as being on par with mine. So I went ahead and awarded this to you in the form of a special ability.

*　　*　　*

Are you saying you're making these special abilities yourself…?

——That's right. After all, this job is so unusual that you are apparently the only one in the entire world to have it. So everything about this job is trial and error on my part.

What kind of special ability is *this?* was all I could think, but it must've been his way of acknowledging me.

◇

It would take a long time until the castle was complete, but I didn't wait for that before officially moving to Maust. For the time being, I set up my base on a hill on the outskirts of Maust. It had quite a different feel than the waterfront castle I would later move into, but it wasn't so bad, either. From there I had a good view of the town as it developed.

"There you are, darling. I was wondering where you were." Seraphina came and stood next to me. A pleasant breeze was blowing, too.

"Watching from afar doesn't finish the work any faster, but it really is fun."

"I know what you mean. Still, you started the construction at a good time. If you did it after unifying the prefecture, I think it would've made things harder by provoking other lords your size."

"Yeah. And the only reason I'm able to hire people from the rest of the prefecture is because I'm not in a big war." I ran my hand through Seraphina's hair as it fluttered in the wind. I thought she'd become far more beautiful than she'd been when I'd first met her in Mineria.

"You're more charming than ever, darling. From every angle, you're a great lord I can be proud of."

"What a coincidence. I was just thinking you look lovelier than ever, too."

"Women are prettier when there's a gentleman they love." Now that we were alone together, we naturally started to fawn on each other. "Actually, darling, I was looking for you because I had something important to tell you."

"Something important?" I started to brace myself. "Not in a bad way, I hope?"

"Just the opposite. It's a very good thing."

What could it be?

"Did your father have a major victory or something?" At that, Seraphina made a show of puffing out her cheeks.

"It's about the two of us." That made it easy enough to figure out.

No way, no way…

"A-are you pregnant?"

Seraphina nodded shyly.

"You did it, Seraphina!" I embraced her straightaway. I'd been a bit worried about not having an heir. But that worry was now gone. "Is it a boy or a girl?"

"You know there's no way to be sure yet. But either way, I'll raise them so they could be confident as a monarch. Because I believe you'll be king, darling."

"True. I won't be satisfied with just one prefecture." I'd end this war-torn era by my own hand. In the middle of my teens, I'd always worried about when I'd die in war. To make it so no one had to think about such pitiful things, someone had to reunify the kingdom. To that end, I'd most likely have to experience many large wars…but I'd do it. There were sixty prefectures in the kingdom. My unification project wasn't even one-sixtieth complete yet. "Well, you need to take it easy for a while. Be very, very careful about your health." It wasn't uncommon for women to die from complications while giving birth. Childbirth was a woman's battle against death.

"Don't worry. My profession is Saint. I'm sure the baby will be protected by the gods."

"I'm worried about the child, but your health worries me, too." I needed to have her offer every prayer in the book at a temple later. But just fretting right now wouldn't do any good. This was a time for joy.

"I'll let my top vassals know right away that you're absolutely not to be bothered...... Oh, right, speaking of my top vassals..."

Laviala's face came to mind first. She definitely would be happy about the pregnancy, but telling her was almost like rubbing it in... As a half-elf, she'd long been unable to get pregnant with my child. I'd heard it was more difficult for someone with elven blood to have children, although I didn't know whether there was any truth to it. Maybe it was because elves were young for a longer time than humans, so the same number of children would cause problems. Still, I couldn't not say anything, so I called for Laviala.

I summoned Laviala to the count's office. Hearing a *knock-knock*, I knew it was her. I could tell right away who it was by the sound of the knock. We really had known each other nearly forever. Since I'd lost both my parents long ago, she had to be the person who'd spent the most of my life with me.

"Come in, Laviala."

"What could this be about? The irrigation canals are coming along nicely. It's great to have dwarf workers who are good at digging, with the town being next to the river."

"Oh, this isn't about work... Ah, right, stay there, please..." I thought it'd be disrespectful to Laviala to say this sitting down, so I got up from my work desk, too. I stood directly in front of her. "That reminds me: When did I get taller than you?"

"What are you on about, all of a sudden...? Um, I think I was bigger until around twelve years old." She might have actually remembered more about me than I did. You see, since it was a wet nurse's job to provide milk, a woman had to be lactating already to be one. Thus, Laviala had been born before me, so sometimes her perspective of me was more a big sister's than a vassal's. Actually, for me, too, I'd seen her as a sister longer than I had a vassal. "Back then you weren't so good with a bow, either. Even in sword practice, I usually beat you, didn't I?"

"Hey, you don't need to bring that up..."

"Didn't you wet yourself in surprise one time when I swung at you with a wood sword? I'm going to laugh again just remembering it."

"Oh, stop. You're going to hurt my dignity as a count taking it that far!" Our eyes met, and we laughed—more as brother and sister than as lord and vassal. Laviala was always proper, though, so she still didn't speak crudely.

"But after that, you improved so quickly. Your body got big to match, too, and two years after that, I could never win against you with a sword."

"But then you went and specialized in the bow instead, and now you're a terror with it." Just talking with Laviala made me feel sentimental. Without her, I surely wouldn't have been able to make it this far.

"You did so well to support Altia when she was sick without your parents, and you suffered so much. Even your success now didn't blossom from nothing; it's thanks to those days you spent in the dirt."

She spoke like a true elf, putting it like that. I was indebted to her family, the Aweyus, too. Actually, you could say they were the only ones who'd looked after Altia and me. The elven Aweyus were Laviala's mother's family. Her father, a human, had died of sickness at about fifty. And Laviala was his last child.

"So then, Lord Alsrod, just what was it you needed me for?" She tilted her head and gazed up at me with puppy-dog eyes.

Oh right. I had an important purpose here. I didn't only want to reminisce.

"I'll announce this sooner or later, but I wanted to tell you first."

"I see. Thank you, Lord Alsrod."

"Don't thank me before hearing it..." I was sure she'd congratulate me. She probably wouldn't even betray the slightest sadness. But surely she worried somewhere in her heart that it was hard for half-elves to get pregnant? As her husband, it bothered me. At least, in my mind I was her husband.

"It might be hard to say, but please just say it, Lord Alsrod."

All right. It's time to tell her.

"Laviala, Seraphina is with child. We're going to have a baby."

"R-really?!" She opened her big eyes even more. Apparently, it was quite a shock.

"I wouldn't lie about something like this. I only just heard a while ago. I'm not sure of the gender, but they'll be a potential heir for now."

"I see. That's really, really good to hear. I'm relieved myself."

"I didn't realize you were so worried, too." In retrospect, it didn't seem as if I'd needed to be so anxious about telling her. I felt immensely relieved.

"Now I can tell you something I couldn't before, too..."

"Huh?! What do you mean by that...?" That was the first I'd heard of this. Well, if she couldn't say it before, of course I hadn't heard, but still. I couldn't believe there was something she was keeping from me. I was sure I had a perfect grasp of her habits and personality.

Surely it couldn't be...that she had another man, could it...? Laviala's looks left nothing to be desired. Her mother—that is, my nurse—was herself famed among elves for her beauty. I was sure all my vassals knew about our relationship, but it was hard to say no one had given in to temptation and made a move.

"Well, here goes..." Laviala's face flushed red—not as if she'd done anything wrong but rather as if she was overjoyed. "Actually, I seem to have been blessed with your child, too, since just the other day."

For a second I wasn't sure what I was hearing. "H-h-huh...? My child...? You must be joking...?"

"I wouldn't joke about something like this." Laviala smiled, saying essentially what I had before.

"Thank you, Laviala!" Before I knew it, I was hugging her. First Seraphina, now Laviala! There couldn't be a happier day than this!

"The other day I was feeling sick, and when I told my mother, she said it was a sign of pregnancy..." I could feel the relief in her voice. "Really I wanted to tell you right away, but I kept quiet for the sake of your wife, Lady Seraphina... I knew she'd been hoping for a child with you..."

"Oh hell, we were all tiptoeing around each other." Apparently, this was what happened when you had multiple wives. But we didn't need to worry about that anymore. "Laviala, this is my order to you as your lord. Whatever you do, have a healthy child. And stay healthy yourself to raise it. All right?"

"Yes, sir! Consider it done!"

In this moment, in this land, no one could have been happier than I. "By the way, will you be the wet nurse for Seraphina's child, too? You can say no if you don't want to." It was just a faint hope that Laviala could dote on Seraphina's child, too, if she raised them together. I was sure Laviala wouldn't play favorites, and there wasn't any worry about matching personalities with a baby. Of course, I realized this was all easy for a man to say.

"Yes, sir! I won't let you down!"

"And if you are tired from work, take a rest. You and this child are more important, you know."

"I'll be fine for a while yet. I can manage until Maust Castle is ready for us to work in at least."

I hugged Laviala tightly once more.

A few days later, I announced to my vassals that Seraphina and my concubine, Laviala, had conceived. Of course, I'd told Altia about it even sooner—in fact, she'd already learned about it from Laviala apparently.

"I'm so glad you're going to have a baby." Altia's relief was almost over-the-top. "If something had happened to you, then I'd be the one to take your place."

"Wait, did you really mean to?" Her health may have improved as of late, but surely she couldn't handle that much.

"Well, you don't know till you try." Altia swung an invisible sword around. Apparently, she wasn't entirely joking. The idea of leaving the Nayvil family to her sure made me feel uneasy, though, so I'd do what I could for now.

News of the pregnancy spread, and for a while, we received what felt like an endless stream of well-wishers—so many that I had to deal with them myself. Otherwise it'd be too exhausting for both Laviala and Seraphina. With my larger territory, there were more people coming to see me than ever; Maust, especially, with all its change, stood out for how many merchants were trying to get authorization for this or that.

I guess being a father is more work than it might seem…

© Kaito Shibano

As I received well-wishers and asked temples everywhere to pray for a safe birth, the construction of Maust Castle made great progress. It'd still take more time to build all the facilities, but the main building was mostly finished. Until it was complete, I'd deal as amicably as possible with the nearby powers so as to avoid any unnecessary conflicts. Most of the remaining independent lords in the north of Fordoneria had sent well-wishers, so they were probably concerned, themselves.

Currently, the Rentrant clan of Nagurry Prefecture to the north was my biggest fear, though the three counties in north Fordoneria just happened to form a buffer zone, so we still weren't directly connected. I'd had good old Commander Kivik build a small castle, so I was ready for an emergency, but for now the situation remained peaceful.

In the midst of all of this, a messenger came from a lord in Olbia, the prefecture south of Fordoneria. All of Olbia was steep and mountainous, preventing the establishment of an overall authority and causing the individual basins to act as separate powers. However, the Olbians had a militaristic spirit about them; they'd be no pushovers if it came to war.

The messenger who came represented the viscount ruling Tacti and Naaham, two counties not directly bordering us. The viscount's family name was Naaham, same as the county. The messenger was a cat-eared therianthrope—no surprise there, since many cat-eared therianthropes were nomadic merchants with no permanent home. Naturally, some of them went on to be appointed as commanders or vassals, and some filled the role of messenger.

"I have come in hopes of forming a military alliance between the two of us." The messenger showed quite a bit of confidence. An unskilled messenger would reflect badly on his lord, so whom to send was a crucial decision. "Currently, the Naaham clan rules two counties, but we are gradually expanding by invading other basins. Lord Brando Naaham, barely eighteen years old, is in the middle of strengthening our country, just as you are."

"Yes, I've heard Viscount Naaham has been doing some brilliant work, and after becoming head of his clan at the tender age of twelve." I was familiar with the name Brando Naaham. Apparently, he was trying to unify Olbia—a difficult task, considering the prefecture's many mountains.

"I presume you are considering an assault to the north, sir. That will eventually lead you to the royal capital, and it's not impossible you could climb to the rank of regent or chancellor."

I chuckled and avoided giving a straight answer. They had read me like an open book. The easiest way to get to the royal capital in the east would be to take Nagurry Prefecture and push onward from there. If I controlled Nagurry, there'd also be a sharp increase in the number of troops I could field. Without lots of troops, I wouldn't be able to defeat the forces around the capital city should they try to stop me. The area around the capital was an agriculturally advanced region, and as a result, the population was greater than in the countryside. Thus, so was the number of troops. One prefecture there, if unified, could provide more than ten thousand troops, according to one story. The people in that area weren't actually united as one, but if people with that much power were to ally, the way to the capital would be shut.

"Indeed, it would be an honor to support the royal family, but what you speak of is unthinkable." I didn't need to admit what I was really thinking, so I said what sounded proper instead.

"Currently, the royal house is split down the middle. If you could bring them together, you would be the most esteemed vassal in the kingdom; I daresay it wouldn't be out of the question for you to be endorsed as the king, either. This is all just my opinion, of course."

Being handed the throne by the royals themselves? That would be amazing, but no lord had ever succeeded at that.

"I'll take that as a compliment. I've never even thought of doing something so insolent as seizing the throne for myself."

——Liar. You were saying you'd be king.

Quiet, you. Some things I just need to keep closer to my chest.

——Sorry, sorry. No, I know all about that. Besides, these things depend on the situation, you know. Back when I had just become head of my clan, I wanted little more than to be of help to Lord Yoshiteru, the thirteenth shogun.

True, if a king was particularly smart, then there wasn't anything to take advantage of.

——It wasn't until after Lord Yoshiteru was killed and I had come up with a way to escort his younger brother to the capital that I really thought I could seize power. Even then, I slowly and gradually did so over time. Until I had at least the same social rank as the shogun, I absolutely didn't kill him even when I had the opportunity; even after exiling him, I planned to install his son as shogun.

In other words, be discreet. It wouldn't be any fun if I did something to warrant someone's envy. I had to bury my feelings deep down, sharing them only with Laviala and Seraphina, at most.

"We presume that you would want to secure your southern border in preparation for the things ahead, so today I am here to discuss an alliance. For the benefit of us both, I certainly would ask for your consideration."

It wasn't a bad proposal, to be sure. It was best to keep your enemies on one flank as much as possible. I sent the messenger away for the time being, telling him I'd think about it. I hadn't even been considering the south as a route, so if anything, it would've come later.

Actually, I'd had another good idea for making an alliance, though part of me hesitated to bring it up. Deciding to think it over with a walk,

I went out to the courtyard. There, Seraphina and Altia were playing airball, a game in which you used a wooden racket to hit a ball back and forth across a net in the middle without letting it hit the ground. As I entered the courtyard, Altia had just jumped in front of the net and hit the ball to Seraphina's side—a well-executed block.

"You're so good at this, Miss Altia!" said Seraphina.

"I'm a thinker. If you hit it so they can only hit it back to a certain spot, it'll be easier to defend." Altia looked a bit smug.

"Hey, hey, Seraphina, don't overdo it with the baby on the way…"

"I can't get out much, so I'm just getting a little exercise. I'm not jumping around like Miss Altia, so don't worry." True—she wasn't even breaking a sweat. Apparently, she'd hardly moved from one spot throughout the entire game. Altia, on the other hand, was sweating after quite some effort.

"You're looking pretty healthy yourself, Altia." Her illness had cleared up recently; the color was even back in her face.

"Yes, Brother. Now I won't be a burden to you any longer."

"I've never thought of you as a burden." Altia was practically my only family. I had other relatives, but I couldn't really open up with them. A relative could potentially supplant me as count, after all.

"But I'm still living here with you." It was easy to tell what she was hinting at. *She really is a nobleman's daughter,* I thought to myself. It was nice to see her so ready, but it also made me feel a bit lonely. Placing her hands on her chest, she continued resolutely, "I'm ready for you to marry me off somewhere." I gazed into Altia's eyes. The little girl, so sick she might fall apart if you touched her, was gone. Anyone would be happy to wed a count's sister like her. I'd never seen her eyes so full of determination.

"Actually, I was just thinking about that, too."

"Maybe the Rentrant family in Nagurry Prefecture to the north? Their heir should be about thirty years old by now."

I wasn't sure whether we ought to discuss this in the courtyard of all places, but it wasn't really something that needed to be hidden.

"Definitely not. I might have to attack Nagurry eventually." Generally when a wife had come from a state that later became an enemy, the marriage ended in divorce, but sometimes she stayed and fought along-side her husband and children. I believed some of these couples even died together. Apparently, those were mostly the ones who were truly in love, though. I could certainly catch Nagurry off guard by sending Altia, but I wanted to avoid using her as a pawn for a surprise attack.

"Then Lady Seraphina's family in the west?"

"Hmm. That's a possibility for strengthening our alliance even more, but it doesn't have much potential to take us anywhere new. We've already managed to build a good relationship." Still, Altia had a pretty good grasp of the goings-on around us.

"Then south... Perhaps the Naaham family in Olbia? Like that young gentleman Brando Naaham."

"Bingo. I was just wondering if it was worth marrying you to him."

Altia seemed to be thinking it over for a while, when finally, slapping her racket against her left hand, she said, "You don't know if a ball is good until you hit it," as if it were some sort of proverb. "To tell if someone is worth marrying, you have to invite them over and see for yourself."

"Like brother, like sister—you two have the same personality," Seraphina said, half-shocked, half-impressed; I knew exactly what she meant.

"Well, what reason should we give for inviting him? I can't really tell him to come to give his appraisal of you. There's other domains between us, even if they're not at war with each other."

"How about asking him to come play airball with the count's sister?" Altia suggested, picking up the ball and softly batting it at me with the racket. I caught it in my right hand; it was quite heavy. "I'm rather good at it."

I accidentally laughed out loud. "Fine. Let's try your idea! Let's invite this Brando Naaham." It made sense. If he didn't have the courage to come all the way through other lords' land just to play airball, he wouldn't pass muster. He wanted to form a military alliance anyway. "Besides, I want to see with my own eyes if he's really good enough to make you his wife."

"You may be cold when it comes to strategy, but you are extremely soft on Miss Altia," commented Seraphina.

"Men are always that way with cute girls. Otherwise they should just be monks—no matter what profession they're bestowed at the temple."

◇

After writing Brando Naaham a letter, I heard back that he'd come right away. He arrived in my territory without incident after paying a hefty toll to the domains he passed through on the way. The two of us met in the temporary castle grounds on the hill in Maust.

"Nice to meet you. I am Brando Naaham, viscount of two counties, including Naaham County." True to the rumors, Brando was a man with a striking look in his eyes. He seemed ready for anything; you could tell how clever he was just by the way he looked at you. But his countenance struck me as more of a leader's than a hero's.

"What profession did you receive at your bestowal ceremony, Lord Brando?"

"The temple bestowed me with Thief. I've won many battles since by sending troops where my enemy's defenses were thin; perhaps that is my own Thief-like intuition at work." It was said that Thief improved judgment by 30 percent over normal people, as well as agility by 50 percent. It was easy to see how it could make someone sharp-witted. Of course, this man had been going to war as clan leader since long before he received his profession, so it seemed more likely it was all down to his own wits.

"I see. It might sound insulting to tell a noble that Thief befits him, but I do think it is your calling."

"I agree. Well then, where is your sister?"

"She's waiting in the yard. I'll show you the way."

Altia was there, wearing a shorter dress than usual. "I will not hold back one bit, Lord Brando," she warned.

The airball match between Altia and Brando Naaham ended in his victory. He really did move with the nimble steps of a Thief. It might've been lazy of me to judge a person's character just from a ball game, but this man was thinking several moves ahead. If you added leadership ability on top of that, he certainly wouldn't be outclassed by any small-time lords. They didn't think about anything but defending themselves anyway.

Right after the match ended, Brando came to me where I'd been watching and bowed his head. "Please, I would like to take your sister as my wife. There is no woman of her beauty in all of Olbia. I am enchanted by her elegance."

To think he'd come to ask me himself. I probably wouldn't have wanted to give my sister to some fool who just went home saying "Thanks for the game!" anyway, though. I glanced at Altia. She nodded slowly. It seemed she'd already made up her mind.

"Very well. However, I won't lend you any troops just for my sister. I have more than enough enemies to fight on my own. Do what you can to make me proud."

"Thank you very much, sir!" He smiled broadly, from ear to ear you might say, and promptly lowered his head.

"Also, don't do anything to make Altia cry. She's already been through more than most people. I want to make things easy for her."

"Yes, sir! You have my promise!"

"I'll send her your way soon. Worry not."

Thus, an alliance with the Naaham clan was formed.

——That Brando is like Azai Nagamasa, another young commander I once knew. He had enough territory to just about warrant being called a daimyo—another reason they're alike. Oichi seemed pretty happy, herself.

Oda Nobunaga seemed somewhat sentimental just then.
So you married off your younger sister, too. Guess that's typical of any lord.

——The situation turned quite thorny when he betrayed me, however. I almost lost my home. I managed to destroy him later on.

Geez, what about your sister, then…?

*   *   *

——I rescued her and her daughters. But she was heartbroken for the rest of her days.

I'm going to make absolutely sure nothing like that ever happens. I want my sister to be happy just as much as I want to be king.

——Well, just be as careful as you can. A king isn't someone who has everything, but someone who sacrificed everything to be king.

That night, Altia and I watched the moon together. We had everyone leave the yard before we sat at a table to drink tea.

"The moon is so gorgeous tonight, Brother." Her mouth hung open slightly as if in a sigh.

"Sure is. I know I should be happy you're getting married, but for some reason I just can't manage it. Maybe that makes me a bad brother."

"No, never!" Altia insisted. "I would've died long ago if you hadn't fretted over me so much. Moving to the hill manor was what helped me get better."

"And if I didn't have you, I'd never have gone to defend that fort like Geisel ordered. We'd probably have surrendered to Mineria, and by now I'd just be leading a single company of troops, at the most." Indeed, if it hadn't been for Altia, I wouldn't have needed to go risk my life defending Fort Nagraad. And if I hadn't done that, an entirely different life would've been waiting for me. My life as a count was thanks to her.

"If I hadn't been your little sister, I'd have wanted to marry you," Altia joked with a laugh.

"I sure would've wanted to marry a woman like you, too."

"I'm so thankful that you raised me, Brother."

"Then you had better be as happy as you can, or else I'll never forgive you, 'kay?"

Afterward, when I was taking her back to her room, she hugged me tightly. I could tell she was crying. "Let it out; cry all you want." It was just as sad for me as for her. I quietly wished for her future happiness.

You're destined to be the sister of a king. Just you wait.

◇

After Altia went off to get married, I devoted myself more than ever to the urban development of Maust. The population had grown beyond what I'd anticipated, so I needed to expand the town area more than originally planned. To that end, I decided to extend the town up to the vicinity of the castle on the hill where I was working. However, since it realistically was hard to run smaller water channels that far, I decided to use one big sideways channel to split the area into River Town, closer to the river, and Hill Town, closer to the hill. It was all one city, if you looked at the big picture, or you could see it as two next to each other.

And finally, about six months after construction began, I moved into Maust Castle. It was normally connected to the castle town by bridge, but if you took that away, it became a citadel sitting entirely within the river.

First, I assembled my vassals in the great hall of the new castle. It was bigger than any room I'd had in Nayvil Castle, but with the increase in my number of vassals, it still didn't look very spacious.

"Gentlemen, from this day forward, this place shall be our political center, economic center, and center of everything else. Not everything may be familiar just yet, but I'm sure you'll come to love it. It's every bit as good as Nayvil Castle in its construction, at least."

My vassals listened respectfully: Laviala with her gradually swelling belly; the veteran commander Kivik, my long-supportive general; the Red Bears, headed by Captain Orcus; likewise, the White Eagles, headed by Captain Leon; the intrepid general Noen, who'd come to work for me after the fall of the former clan he'd served; Fanneria, the werewolf financial officer; and Ornis, a Maustian ex-merchant.

The rest of my retainers consisted of various individuals gathered here from many different lands. Longtime senior vassals of the Nayvil family were among them, albeit not enough to be the majority.

"Now then, let me tell you about a certain goal of mine. Feel free to laugh if you still think these are mere delusions of grandeur. However, I

137

do intend to make this particular delusion a reality. When I was lord of but three small villages, I had plans to take over the territory that is now in my possession; what I'm going to do next isn't so different." I paused for a beat before continuing, "Currently, the royal family is in utter chaos. Their line is split in two, with powerful top vassals and clans on both sides. Each faction has made a scene of taking the capital from the other several times. As a resident of the Kingdom of Therwil, I find it most reprehensible. And so..." I looked my vassals in the face, one by one. None of them seemed to think I was being delusional.

"...I will go to the capital and help the fallen royal family recover. Serving at the side of the king, I will end the chaos in this country."

More than likely, about half of them probably thought I wanted to take power by making the king my puppet—plenty of others had done so in the past. Close, but not quite. I was aiming even further ahead: I would make my own kingdom. Of course, it wouldn't be easy, but my territory had already grown roughly six times its size since I'd become head of my clan. If I could expand it another six times over, not many could win against that.

"So I want you all to work your hardest. It won't be an easy road, but I'll reward you as best I can. Some of you could easily end up with a whole county—nay, a whole prefecture. Work with that in mind. Now let's raise our voices together, shall we?" I grabbed that long spear, the one I'd gotten from the cathedral. It was proof that I was at the top of this prefecture, in both might and authority.

I tapped the floor with the butt of the spear. "Glory to our realm!"

""Glory!"" The new castle was filled with their voices.

At the same time, another voice echoed inside my head:

Special ability Conqueror's Aura activated.
As long as an individual with this profession resides in his castle as a conqueror, he and his family will age at an extremely slow rate.

Looks like I got something new.

Does family include my wives? It'd be nice if Seraphina and Laviala kept their beauty.

——Can't you be more excited? After I went out of my way to bestow this upon you—how disappointing.

Expanding my territory is more important than something like that. First I'll unify the prefecture by taking the three counties left in the north.

——Ah, the place with all the smaller lords. I can't wait to watch.

Not sure if you'll like what you see, but have fun.

I assembled the Red Bears and White Eagles, as well as the elite units led by Kivik and Noen.

"A lord of one of the three counties not under my control is being uncooperative. We're going to eliminate him and his forces. First, capture that fort of his. Let me be clear: Kill them all. Don't let anyone in that fort out alive."

"My lord, may I ask for clarification?" asked Noen Rowd. Still in his midthirties, he was a warrior in the prime of his career. He had served under some useless lord originally, but after I'd handily destroyed him, Noen had come to work for me. "With the enemy close to a village this time, there may be some nearby residents taking refuge with them, making it difficult to tell them apart. In that case—"

"You may kill anyone in the fort," I replied plainly. "I've already sent word to both the village and their lord, saying, 'We will kill everyone in the fort. This is not just a threat.' If they're still hiding in the fort, I'll consider them combatants."

"Understood. As long as I know, that's fine by me." Noen nodded. "Also, as far as how to capture the fort, shall we surround them and try to wait them out slowly? That would be the usual strategy anyway."

"Don't you know why I brought you all here? Just overpower them and take it."

"Y-yes, sir…" Noen nodded again, a bit timidly this time.

"Since you don't all yet seem to understand my intentions, I'll explain. If you eradicate your enemies all at once in the first battle, what'll happen to the ones waiting elsewhere?"

The veteran commander Kivik stepped forward. "I think most of them would be too afraid to fight," he said. "If they're peasant troops, they'll probably try to desert."

"Exactly. If we show them in the first fight how much stronger we are, the enemy will quickly submit. If the first battle goes well, we can subjugate their lord without any more battles." So even if it wasn't easy, I'd crush the first fort. I'd make them see that my forces were of a different quality than anyone they'd faced before. "Besides, if the war drags on, they'll call in more-troublesome enemies. I'd like to avoid that."

"You mean Colt Rentrant of Nagurry." With his abundance of experience, Kivik sure was sharp. The lords of the three remaining counties had always been friendly with the Rentrants in Nagurry. That was how the smaller lords guaranteed their security.

"It's never been my goal to unify the prefecture by eliminating these minor lords. My goal is to eliminate the Rentrants in Nagurry. This fight…is no more than the first step." That astonished my troops. They probably had never imagined unifying the prefecture, much less taking other prefectures. After all, for the longest time, no one had ever appeared who could.

One man among them, however—Captain Leon of the White Eagles—spoke up: "Bravo." He went on to add, "You're thinking further ahead than anyone else, my lord. That's why I'll follow you anywhere."

I wanted my imperial guard at the very least to understand my—Oda Nobunaga's—thinking. *The more you try for the top, the lonelier you are*, I thought.

Must be why so few tried.

I brought my troops to the enemy lord's fort. His troops were positioned on a small hillock—probably about a hundred or so of them. I say a fort, but it was a long way from being a proper stone fortress. There was something like a stone wall surrounding the hill, but if you got over that, you could breach the fort itself.

"With your skill, you lot can do this with brute force, no problem. Well, who should I pick to go in first?" It went without saying that the men spearheading the attack were in the most danger.

"Leave it to me!" Noen Rowd piped up. "I made a shameful display of myself the other day, not understanding your intentions. I would like to atone for that."

This man has quite a future, I thought. Originally serving as a general to another clan, which I had destroyed, he had quite a devoted personality. "Well said. All right, then—see what you can do. I'll give you just a few hints, though." I described several weak points in the enemy's defenses. "...And so from the north, it'll be simple to get up to the fort. This fort was made with defense against southern attacks in mind; they assumed they could run north toward their main stronghold if they couldn't hold against a southern attack. Naturally, the road that way isn't as steep."

"Only you could figure out so much so quickly...," marveled another general.

"If you put yourself in the enemy's shoes, the answer is obvious. Now it's your turn, Noen."

"Yes, sir! We shall crush them without fail!"

Noen's men immediately set out for the rear of the fort. The rest of us gathered on the fort's south side, drawing away the enemy's attention. Before long, I could hear the screams when Noen's unit entered the fort.

"All right, Kivik, the enemy will try to flee toward us. Block their path and destroy them."

"As you wish! We won't let a single one out alive!"

Some of the enemy soldiers leaped out, trying to escape. Since there probably weren't many troops highly loyal to such a minor lord, it was hardly a surprise.

Sorry, but you're all going to die here and now.

"Ready your bows. Shoot anyone who comes out!"

Realizing they had no means of escape, the enemy troops ran as fast as they could, trying to force their way out of the encirclement. They felt more like running than fighting now. Still, I showed no mercy and ordered them slain one after another. We had the Tri-Jargs lined up here, after all. It'd be no simple task to break through their formation. Seeing so many spearpoints in a row, the enemy troops stopped in their tracks. Now that their momentum was gone, there was no longer anything to fear from them.

Smoke finally rose from the fort. Noen had done it. "We've won! Now, just one more thing to do to make our victory complete!"

Seeing the overwhelming victory, our troops let out a cheery cry of "Raaah!" In the end, the battle was finished after only a few hours of actual fighting.

Noen was covered in dirt when he got back, but he seemed unhurt. "My lord, we have killed the enemy general. He was their lord's younger brother. Apparently, he was begging for his life, but we slaughtered him anyway."

"Good. What a pathetic wretch, begging for his life at the very last minute."

Begging for his life right before the fort fell, after I went to the trouble of warning them I'd kill everyone there?

"These people seem to have no respect for battle," Captain Leon of the White Eagles remarked. "Even in this age, they haven't seen a real eye-for-an-eye bloodbath. These lesser lords have been depending on each other for everything, never knowing a truly horrific war."

"Leon, you used to be a mercenary for the elves, didn't you?"

"Yes, and many of their lords were just as naive. It wasn't uncommon for them to never have any real accomplishments in battle."

"You would seem to be right. But past matters like that don't make a difference to me. I'm not going to relent."

——Yes, very good. Crush any who get in your way.

Now that you mention it, you seem like you'd hate slow fights, yourself.

——Battle is the most effective opportunity to demonstrate your power, you know. I almost never staged a siege. In a lengthy skirmish, no one gets a sense for the attacker's might, even if you wait out the enemy and get them to surrender. Not to mention if you give up the siege, you're hurt by the loss. And it takes time.

I feel the same way. If you can defeat your enemy outright, then you should.

——With what you've done here, you should be able to eliminate this lord, too. If he's a fool, this fort's extermination will make him so afraid that he'll offer to surrender. Fools have no courage. There's no way he's prepared to die a hero's death defending his land.

You're right. I can't wait to see his reaction.

Before long, their lord offered his surrender, so I ordered him to visit me at my camp. I could tell he was useless by the way he looked. His belly was protruding so much you couldn't possibly call him a warrior. Holing up here in the countryside, he'd probably never done any real diplomatic negotiations. I'd thought his spirit of defiance might be useful for something, but this wouldn't work at all.

"My lord, I admit I was wrong; please forgive me... Please, please..."

He was desperately trying to save himself by apologizing over and over. He should've heard before of our power and numbers, so what was he doing bowing before me now? Though, Oda Nobunaga said there were lots of lords without foresight when he was conquering, too—fighting just because they didn't want to surrender, only to finally see their own folly.

"Very well; I'm no brute. I'll forgive you. We haven't directly crossed swords with you, after all. You won't be a target for extermination."

"Thank you very much! I shall serve you here, with my very life!"

"You don't understand, do you?" I said coldly. "I'm going to have my own vassal govern this place. Your clan can go live as peasants in a village near Nayvil."

"Wh-what?! But you said you would forgive me…"

"Well, I spared your life, didn't I? Don't worry. I'll take your vassals for myself and reorganize them." With a leader like this, the vassals would have practically no loyalty. No particular backlash was likely. "Take him away." Some men, burly even for my guard troops, took the now ex-lord by the arms and pulled him away.

Well, guess I'll take down the remaining lords.

I sent an ultimatum to the other minor lords. It basically went as follows:

Fordoneria Prefecture has only one count—Alsrod Nayvil. It is therefore only logical that all other lords obey Alsrod and devote themselves to serving him as vassals.

The most recent lord was deposed by Lord Alsrod for his lack of cooperation. This is not to say that those defeated by the count who surrendered in fear became his allies; their territory was subsequently confiscated. Of course, anyone who promptly pledges to serve Alsrod will be given appropriate treatment as his vassal.

Feel free to fight if you wish, but be prepared to lose your ancestral lands. After all, why fear losing your land when a war could cost you your very life?

Immediately, four lords brought hostages and submitted. Only three places left, then. I went to put them down, but it wasn't a real fight in the end. Even if individual lords tried to resist, not all their vassals agreed with such a decision in the first place.

"I have come to serve you, my lord!"

"I have forsaken my liege to come to you!"

One after another, vassals came to me with such greetings.

I knew this already, but a lord's vassal is really just a lower lord himself. Many would elect to leave their liege to save themselves. I promised to treat such ones graciously. When word thus got out that obeying me was beneficial, suppression became even easier.

In the end, even a top vassal serving the Branchovs, a viscount-level clan, came to swear fealty to me. Though, with only about a third of a county in territory, he may have just been calling himself a viscount.

"My family was originally a branch of the Branchovs; we have performed our duty for about a hundred years."

"Wow, you must have quite some resolve to abandon your master from a position like that. I'm genuinely pleased." There was no deceit in my words. If such an important vassal left his lord, the other vassals would definitely be shaken. Surely more people would give up further resistance.

"If this lord can be subjugated, I wouldn't mind giving you an appropriate reward. My enemy will have lost his right-hand man without need for a battle."

"Yes, sir! Though, I would certainly like to show tangible proof of my desire to serve you, so I came bearing a gift."

This man seemed to have plenty of confidence. *He must've brought me something quite nice*, I thought. I wasn't sure even a senior vassal of a small lord would have anything of great worth, but the attendant waiting at his side was holding some sort of box.

"Please take a look." The attendant opened the box. Inside was a head—two, in fact. "As proof of my loyalty, I have brought to you the severed heads of the viscount and his heir! The Branchov clan is already practically dead! Behold, my own personal token of fealty to you, my lord!"

Hey, Oda Nobunaga? Are you there?

——Don't only call for me whenever you feel like it! Anyway, I'd overlook it. Conquerors look kindly on those who amuse them.

So am I wrong to want to murder this man?

——Actually, I did something similar once. Right before the great daimyo Takeda was defeated, one of his senior vassals, Oyamada Nobushige, came to me and announced he'd betrayed his master. I had him and his men put to death. He hadn't told me of any plans to betray his master; he'd simply turned on the man at the last moment. This wasn't a scheme of any sort. He was just a swine violating the laws of decency.

Never thought I'd hear you talk about decency.

——Some called me a monster even in my time, but that's a gross misunderstanding. I always obtained justification when I could. On the battlefield, one can't always afford to worry about what people think, but a person can never seize power if they always insist on being barbaric.

Indeed.

"So I have just one question for you."

"Yes, sir! What might that be? Is it about the Branchovs' land?"

"Do you think I want to have a man who kills his master without even being asked as my vassal?"

He turned pale. "No, I only did this because my master was such a fool... This certainly doesn't mean I'm disloy—"

"I'm not interested in your loyalty. But what I'm saying is that I can't trust you. *Kill him.*" Captain Leon of the White Eagles, who was by my side, slaughtered him then and there—and then his attendants, too. "Thinking he can curry favor doing something like this is itself an insult to me. Did he think I could trust him so quickly just for being my enemy's enemy?!"

Afterward, I took my troops and eliminated what little was left of the Branchovs as well as the remaining two clans. Time after time, the soldiers of most forts my men approached tried escaping, leaving us only with an empty place to occupy. Rumors had spread that anyone opposing me would be massacred. In that case, they shouldn't have tried defending at each fort in the first place, but their commanders must've initially held their ground in an outward show of defending their land. And then they'd lose their nerve after all. Believing their lord would surely fight for them, they'd devise a strategy, only to have it fall apart spectacularly. By capturing that one fort with brute force, no matter the casualties, I now didn't have to fight as many battles, so the number of casualties had seemed to go down.

"My lord, you seem to be a bit down," Orcus of the Red Bears pointed out as we were on the move. As my personal guard, the Red Bears and the White Eagles were often on standby near me.

"Yes, but the war is going well. Ah, right, that must be it." There was one thing missing. "Laviala was pretty much always right at my side. I might be a little off with her not around."

"You haven't had any women around recently to be sure. Shall we go snatch one from a village somewhere for you?"

Leon of the White Eagles immediately shouted, "You should know the Count of Fordoneria isn't going to pillage Fordoneria Prefecture!" That certainly was more reasonable. After all, the enemy's territory was more mine than theirs.

"I'm sure you realize, but anyone found in violation of the elite corps' discipline will be executed, you know."

"Oh, I understand. Feasting on meat is more up my alley than women, anyways," Orcus replied evasively.

At last, I'd closed in on the castle of the last resisting lord in the northern tip of Fordoneria—it belonged to the Wouge clan, a family steeped in tradition. Their lord's castle was just as one might expect from one so close to the border. This place must've worked as a checkpoint between prefectures for about a thousand years. It was sturdy and hard to assault, so I decided to surround it for a few days and see what happened. And partly, I wanted to see whether reinforcements would come from the neighboring Nagurry Prefecture. A besieged army's whole strategy rested on the assumption that reinforcements would come from somewhere, as it was absolutely impossible to win by just defending.

According to spy reports, no troops would be coming from Nagurry anytime soon. They must have realized it was impossible to stop our prefecture's unification this late. As we slowly tightened the noose, the Wouge clan informed us they wanted a conditional surrender. When we told their messenger, "If your clan gives themselves up, the soldiers can live," their clan came out to us from the castle, apparently agreeing.

Thus, my unification of Fordoneria Prefecture was complete. The endeavor itself was over within a month. My subjects wouldn't have been pleased if I'd dragged such a war out or even raised taxes, hence why I'd meant to crush the opposition outright. However, I seemed to remember Oda Nobunaga saying that unifying the first prefecture was surprisingly hard, and now I understood what he meant. Including all the different preparations, like moving castles, it had taken quite a long time. Still, it wasn't too bad being lord of a prefecture at the tender age of twenty.

◇

With the conflict in Fordoneria ended, I stayed at an inn for one night and met with my top vassals.

"First, let me thank all of you for your service in this war. The fruits of your labors are countless and magnificent." It must have felt truly amazing for all of them after our triumph. Since I allowed drinking after a victory, some of their faces were red. Orcus of the Red Bears always had a red face anyway, so now he was such a bright hue, it was almost scary.

"In particular, Noen brought us a flawless first victory, which made the rest of the war much easier. We ended up with far fewer enemies that could really stand against us." Noen looked quite proud of himself. For an outsider vassal like Noen, making a big contribution and being recognized for it was an important rite of passage.

"Also, as for treatment of the enemy clan that surrendered, once we've determined who advocated for the war, they'll be executed along with their lord—that's my intent. The rest will be incorporated into our military. The women and children will be sent to Seraphina and made to help her."

Since choosing to hole up meant they'd intended to resist, it'd be reasonable not to forgive them, but I wanted to decide their fate after seeing my vassals' reactions. The last lord I'd fought was named Meissel Wouge; compared to other lords, he had some mettle. Since there hardly seemed to be any who surrendered, he must've had the confidence of his vassals. If he seemed fit to be a general, I wouldn't mind using him.

"If anyone has an opinion, feel free to speak."

"Yessir," said Captain Orcus, raising his hand. "Some of the enemy troops were rather skilled. Let 'em into the Red Bears. They were well-practiced. Besides, this is Fordoneria, after all. It might be good to show some leniency as the Count of Fordoneria."

Oh, Orcus. Hadn't Leon scolded him about this very thing before? "Very well. Do what you will for new recruits."

Noen raised his hand next. "With all due respect, the viscount Meissel Wouge had some backbone. If you could pardon him, I would like to use him as a commander under my banner."

Orcus protested, "You can't have him; he's mine." Warriors always thought the same.

"Orcus, it's your fault for not being specific. There are other promising ones besides Meissel. Be content with them." Orcus backed down. "Also, Noen, your request couldn't have come at a better time." It'd work well with my plan. "Noen, I'm making you commander of the north hill castle that Meissel Wouge was defending." The north hill castle was what everyone called it because it was at the northernmost tip of the prefecture. Looking north from the castle, you could see Nagurry Prefecture at the bottom of the terrace. The castle was officially called Holai Castle. Perhaps because of its important role, even Noen looked a bit overwhelmed.

"I don't have to tell you that it's going to be one of the most crucial spots in the coming war, do I?" I continued. "We'll have to lock it down tight in our battle with Nagurry's Rentrant clan. The enemy will most definitely attack us shortly. Now that I've unified the prefecture sooner than anyone had imagined, the Rentrants must've realized the gravity of the situation."

I'd taken some time to get Maust Castle built, which must've led them to underestimate me. Otherwise, they surely would've actually tried to interfere in the recent battle of unification. Either way, we'd be fighting against Nagurry Prefecture next.

"I'd therefore like to put one of my top vassals in the north hill castle—Holai Castle. However, it'd be careless to send away my guards-men, the Red Bears and White Eagles, and Kivik also—"

"I may be old, but I can still keep up with the youngsters. Compared to my days at Fort Nagraad, this place is like heaven."

I smirked as he reached my point before I did. "I know, but my parents are gone, so I want to take care of the elderly. We'll have to go to war again anyway. Until then, take it easy at Maust Castle."

"I will do whatever you ask." Kivik nodded formally. Incidentally, his son—whom I called Little Kivik—was himself already in his thirties and serving me, though he seemed fed up with his old man's formality.

"So anyway, for now I'm entrusting Noen with full authority in those three counties. Rule it firmly, with carrot and stick. You'll be donning your armor before long anyway."

"I shall make every effort to live up to your expectations..." Noen bowed his head deeply. It was certainly a heavy responsibility, but I was sure it'd make him that much more determined. Kivik was undeniably old, and considering what was to come, I wanted to have more commanders I could use.

"All right. While we're at it, let's call the Viscount of Holai in here."

A while later, Meissel Wouge, Viscount of Holai, was brought in. He was younger than I'd expected, probably about halfway into his twenties. His countenance was submissive from the moment he came in.

"My lord, I am prepared to take responsibility and die for defying you." He hadn't heard yet that he was going to be spared.

"I want to ask one question. You didn't have a chance of winning this fight from the beginning. Why didn't you surrender? Or you could've fled to Nagurry, like some of the other lords." Including the vassals of lords, the number of people who'd abandoned their lands to take refuge with the Rentrants in Nagurry added up to quite a bit.

"My family has ruled this land for generations. I cannot hand it over without even fighting. A lord is above his people because he protects the land with his life. It would be shameful if the ruler of the people fled straightaway."

I see. This man certainly is qualified to be a lord.

"I like you. I want you to work as a commander for Noen Rowd there. I'm going to take away your rank as viscount for now, but if you work hard enough, you might end up with more land than you ever had."

Meissel looked surprised. "I thought people who disobeyed would be killed as a matter of course... That's what you were doing in this invasion."

"That depends on the person. If they're useful, I'll put them to work, and if they're useless, I'll kill them. That's all."

——Yes, yes. As long as they're useful to you, commanders should be used. I forgave Matsunaga Hisahide after he betrayed me once, you know. Of course, he betrayed me again later...

Oda Nobunaga was speaking once again.

——I was going to forgive Araki Murashige, too, but he stubbornly refused to cooperate... Why do people betray me so much...?

I'm not interested in your griping.

——A-anyway, use who you can. Otherwise you won't be able to manage your territory as it grows.

He's right about that.

"I, Meissel Wouge, will work to the best of my ability as thanks for your kindness."

"It's not kindness," I said, laughing. I wasn't that nice. "I'm making use of you because I can. So now it's your turn to show what you're worth. Prove to me why you should exist."

◇

Returning to Maust Castle, I worked to gather intelligence on Nagurry Prefecture. In my spare time, I was constantly thinking about how I should fight against the Rentrants. Thinking about it was actually easier while I was resting in my wife Seraphina's chambers than during my official duties, as I was able to take my mind off work for a bit. This wasn't the sort of thing to ruminate over at all hours. Also, only a few other men aside from myself were allowed in Seraphina's section of the castle, which basically functioned as the consorts' quarters.

"I can't believe you're having a staring contest with the map again, darling," Seraphina said to me as I pored over a map spread out on the table.

"I have to. This is going to be a bigger war than we've ever seen." This'd be the first time I'd fight an opponent of the same size since I'd become the ruler of a prefecture. Failure on our end would spell our doom.

"He can't help it—please bear with it for a bit longer, Lady Seraphina." Laviala came bringing tea. With her position, she didn't need to be acting like a maid, but she'd always been particularly helpful when it came to things like this.

"Both of your bellies sure have grown. I'd like to deal with the Rentrants before our children are born, but that's looking pretty difficult."

"Lord Alsrod, you seem more enthusiastic than ever," Laviala said as she poured me some tea. "Nevertheless, wouldn't it be hard to take a prefecture in only a few months, even for someone so unmatched as you?"

"Yeah. Even Oda Nobunaga said it took him time to conquer Mino, a province near his."

"Oda Nobunaga? You mean your profession?"

"Uh… Never mind."

I didn't want word to spread that I was having conversations with Oda Nobunaga. Not that anyone would believe it anyway. There wasn't a soul who'd considered that a profession could be a person's name to begin with.

——Yes, the problem of how to take your first one or two provinces is truly a vexing one. Generally, most daimyo couldn't manage it. They all had their hands full protecting just one province. Of course, once you expand your territory, you make enemies everywhere, so that brings new problems itself.

Hey, Oda Nobunaga…can you just be quiet right now?

I'd known my profession long enough to understand his personality. And that he liked to talk. He was the type who would've had several biographies or whatnot written about himself if he unified the country. Well, there probably weren't many opportunities to talk about the process of unification, so I did kind of understand how he felt.

As I looked alternately at Laviala and Seraphina, I said, "I mean it when I say I want another prefecture before our children are born. Otherwise, I'd have to think about my kids and the war at the same time, you know."

"You'll have to defeat the enemy quickly, then. You might not even have a moment's reprieve," Seraphina said, giggling. Their due dates really were just beyond the horizon.

"I've pretty much decided on my strategy. I can make my move soon."

I put a check on a spot on the map of Nagurry. I would put myself at an advantage before they attacked.

"Really I'd like to do everything I could for you, darling, but with the baby on the way, I can't be of much help right now."

"As would I," Laviala added.

They looked at each other and said "Right?" in agreement. It seemed the two of them had become closer recently—maybe because they had similar positions.

"But, darling... I've had some of my own worries about you." Seraphina sounded somewhat pained.

"I know; you've always been watching over me. You're my saint, just like your job title."

"No, I mean something more specific. Miss Laviala, if you'd please..." At that, Laviala left the room.

What's this about?

When Laviala came back, she brought a girl along with her. The girl was probably about fifteen years old and had lovely pink hair. She couldn't be one of Seraphina's ladies-in-waiting—her dress was too elegant. I was sure she was quite high-class, but who could she be?

"I believe this is the first time we've properly met." Her voice was pretty, like a tinkling bell.

"Whose daughter are you? If I had a vassal so lovely, I'm sure rumor would've spread quickly."

"I am Meissel Wouge's younger sister, Fleur."

Ah, the lord of Holai Castle's sister.

"Until two years ago, I lived with the Rentrants of Nagurry as a hostage. As such, I believe I may be able to tell you a little bit about their internal affairs."

"That would be helpful. I certainly would like to learn a lot from you."

"Yes, I hope so, as well."

She really seemed well-mannered. Part of her modesty might've been because she was a noble girl from a vanquished clan, though.

Seraphina stepped in between us. "When the Wouge family sent this girl, I thought she might be able to help you. She's very smart, for one, and she's got a trustworthy nature, too."

Fleur placed a hand on her chest, a gesture denoting a vow. "I want to repay you for sparing my family. Besides, I am sure my elder brother will be fighting on the front lines in the next war against the Rentrants. For his sake, too, I would like to ensure that the war goes well. To that end, I shall tell you everything that I can."

Her line of thinking was mostly correct. As proof of their submission, it was customary that lords who surrendered should fight up front in the next war. Of course, they didn't always have to if they were old or more like a civilian.

"I appreciate the sentiment. Would you mind if I went ahead and asked you a few questions?"

"Please, go right ahead. Anything."

"The Rentrants must be preparing for war, themselves, but when would be a good time to attack?" I deliberately asked a sort of test question.

"It may be good to have it coincide with the wheat harvest. They wouldn't be able to levy as many soldiers. Southern Nagurry is particularly fertile and will need hands for some time. However, the land is too flat to be good for defense."

Interesting. She's definitely letting this intel flow freely.

"Well, what sort of reason do you think they have for not attacking?"

"There are several possibilities. First, they might only be thinking about defending their own prefecture. None of Nagurry Prefecture itself has been taken yet." That was entirely plausible. Supposedly lords with abundant land become conservative. "Next, they might want to avoid fighting in Fordoneria. Peasant soldiers don't like going far away. There would be an even greater risk to morale if they had to march all the way to a neighboring prefecture."

"What? Really? I thought for sure they'd be happier to do that than fight on their own land...," said Laviala. "Their farmland wouldn't have to be destroyed, after all..." She seemed confused, though I could understand why.

"If it takes three or four days just to get to the battlefield, a lot of peasant soldiers won't be happy," I said. "Besides, they'll fight desperately when defending their own land, but it'd be a waste of effort for perfectly well-fed soldiers to go all the way to another prefecture unless they managed to take something that was worth it."

"I see… I'd never thought of that before…"

That was another reason why I'd wanted to make professional soldiers who could go fight anywhere. My guard troops the Red Bears and the White Eagles were preparation for that. With troops that could fight in any season, I could attack when the enemy wanted to avoid fighting.

"Lastly…it might be a way to lure you into an ambush." Fleur dragged her finger between several forts on the map. "All the forts in their prefecture are in the backcountry. If the Fordonerian invasion reaches all the way there only to be defeated, retreating would be incredibly difficult. There is a risk your troops may be destroyed in the meantime."

"Miss Fleur, you really are astute," I said. Under the cover of being a hostage, she'd probably also worked to relate the internal affairs of Nagurry to her home country. She was no bird in a cage. I might have just gotten a bigger piece on the board than I'd thought.

As I was admiring Fleur, Seraphina moved to block the map. "Darling, this is my room you're in. Did you know that?"

"Ah, I wasn't thinking. Sorry, sorry."

"That's not what I mean… I just think Miss Fleur's room might be better for your little war council." Seraphina glanced in Laviala's direction.

"Yes, I too think that would be wise…," Laviala said, looking down slightly.

Glancing at their faces, I guessed what they were on about. For me, the lord of the castle, to go to a woman's room in the castle was…well, basically just what it sounded like.

"Miss Laviala and I are pregnant, so we get tired talking for a long time. We'd just like to go to bed for the night. I don't know anything about Nagurry, anyway, so why don't you discuss it with Miss Fleur?" Even though Seraphina was the one suggesting it, she looked a bit forlorn. Most likely, she herself had assigned Fleur as my concubine. I'd been so concerned about Seraphina's and Laviala's feelings that I hadn't chosen any new concubines.

"If you don't mind, Miss Fleur, I'd like to ask you a few more questions."

"I have no objections," Fleur answered quietly, ever the epitome of elegance.

"Well then, let's talk a bit more about where best to penetrate."

Once we'd moved to a different room, I asked one more question. "Does your brother know about this? I'd like to avoid a situation that would offend him."

"He told me before we parted that he has no reason to oppose me join-ing your house. Your wife also asked that I spend the night with you."

Having made her say this much, adding anything more would be uncouth.

"Well, let's not disappoint Seraphina."

And so I made love to Fleur.

I knew right away that Fleur was devoted and brave.

"Fleur, the Wouge family will be safe as long as they obey me. I promise."

"Thank you. Please do treat my family kindly."

She must have spent her life thinking she had the fate of her family resting on her little shoulders. Her expression was a bit stiff. It was the face of someone who knew all too well what obligations a lord had.

I put my hand to her cheek. "You should try to look happier. You may think of yourself as a maiden of a fallen country, but right now no one's going to blame you for smiling."

"Thank you very much. It's been many years since I last heard such kind words..." As if some of her uneasiness up to then had been resolved, Fleur smiled, albeit with a little lingering awkwardness.

"There, that's much cuter." Stroking her hair, I hugged her tight.

A few days later, I officially made Fleur my concubine.

© Kaito Shibano

Maybe I could've been content just gloating about unifying one prefecture, but alas, I wasn't that kind of man. My designs on the northern counties had also been preparation for attacking Nagurry Prefecture.

All the arrangements were in place. I could go into Nagurry anytime now. There were many counts who had one prefecture, but there were far fewer with two or more. In other words, this would be a big step toward being king. And for that reason, I needed to attack far sooner than my enemies would ever expect.

"First, we'll use an advance party to capture Fort Saura in the prefecture's heartland. The fort is situated in the valley of a mountain. It'll come down to a decisive battle nearby."

I gave the conscription order to the whole prefecture, and before all the troops were even assembled, I went north with just a portion of them, including my personal guard. On the way, I went to the north hill castle that Noen ruled, located at the northernmost tip of my prefecture.

"You've come with an awfully small number... You're attacking the neighboring prefecture. I thought you'd come with your whole army..." Noen seemed a bit confused.

"More troops will come gather here as a staging point anyway. We don't need a huge force to take down all the smaller forts. In fact, if we take our time, they'll bring reinforcements." We wouldn't need a lot of troops until later. First we had to go take down their forts, or none of this would work.

Meissel Wouge, basically second-in-command of Holai Castle, came

along, too. "Thank you very much for taking a liking to my sister." Seeing his face so full of determination, it was obvious he was fighting for
his clan's revival. I could tell he really wanted to produce results.

"Your sister helped make this possible. There is no question we will
win this war. Come help the advance party; Noen can take care of this
place himself."

We invaded Nagurry Prefecture with about seven hundred men, capturing a few forts along the way. They were all just small forts meant
to defend against invasion by the small northern lords of Fordoneria;
most of them had essentially been left wide open. Some of them were
completely empty shells. Obviously abandoned forts weren't able to stop
us. The enemy had never imagined someone with a whole prefecture
would come attack in the first place. It struck me that these forts hadn't
been repaired or rebuilt. That must've meant they had no intention of
defending against us on the fringe of their territory.

As we went on, troops who had been lagging behind joined up, making
our total count about a thousand men. With that, we captured Fort Saura
deep in central Nagurry. The fort was on a low mountain, but its soldiers
also fled without much of a fight. Now the real showdown was set to begin.

I held a meeting with my imperial guard. "Now, once we cross a few
mountain passes, we'll be in the flatlands of northern Nagurry. We can
then thrust straight to their main stronghold, Molkara Castle." Molkara
Castle was part of a seaport town. Nagurry Prefecture, with its north
end bordering the ocean, had lots of port towns. "However, there are
many forts before we get through the pass. We've definitely never seen
so many forts so close to each other before. They seem to be undergoing
extensive repairs, as well. You know what this means, don't you?"

Everyone, including Leon and Orcus, nodded. "It means the enemy
wants to isolate and destroy us here. If they flank us from behind this
fort, we'll be caught in a pincer maneuver."

"Leon is correct," I said. "If you read the history books, the same sort
of tactic was used here hundreds of years ago."

"If we try to force our way through now, we'll be weakened by each of the forts, and once we've made it out to the plains, exhausted, their main force will hit us hard. Then even if we retreat, another flanking force can lie in wait for us from behind," Orcus said, holding his hand to his face.

"Exactly. Well, they probably thought we'd have a lot more soldiers in this fort, but still." This area gave a large army nowhere to run. That was why I sent a lot of troops to support our rear. That way, they could take out any separate flanking force. I, too, was using my head. I'd destroy the enemy all at once.

——You seem awfully excited. Well, their lord's castle isn't inland, so I'm sure you can handle it. It'll be easier than my attack on Mino.

You might be right. I've got you on my side, so I'll eliminate my neighbors faster than you did, I said to Oda Nobunaga.

"By the way, how're we gonna attack them? Things'll probably get worse the more we wait around." Orcus had a habit of touching his beard when he was thinking. "If we go down the valley road, we'll get hit by the enemies in the forts ahead. We can't just ignore them and force our way through, so it's gonna be a bit rough."

Yes, this fort, Fort Saura, was right inside of the valley. The enemy was hoping to close us in and destroy us in an encirclement. Just looking at the situation, they must've assumed we'd fallen right into their trap. The enemy lord, Colt Rentrant, was a smart enough man. He could muster more troops than I could, so he was probably thinking of hitting us hard here and then attacking my prefecture for real.

——Speaking of, that sort of thing happened when I was alive as well. The Oouchi troops, led by Sue, were lured to and destroyed in Itsukushima by Mouri Motonari; he then went on to slowly push into Oouchi territory, wiping them out.

Well, I don't plan to let that happen. I'll overcome this.
"Meissel, the map." What Meissel spread out was just a magnification

of the surrounding mountains and valley. "I actually found a few secret passages leading from this fort to theirs beforehand. The path along the ridge is mysteriously blocked, as if you can only go back, but we can go around by going down and back up." I'd gotten that info from my spies and Fleur. "The enemy's strategy assumes we'll be weakened by having to capture each of their forts. If we can take them quickly, we can burst out onto the plain with all our strength left." I looked at their faces. "If the forts ahead are acting as a roadblock, we only need to destroy them ahead of time. Then when we meet up with the task force from behind and go out to the plain, our victory will be sealed."

"I see your intentions, but goin' around takin' forts is awfully reckless, too."

"You're all perfectly capable." These men were being affected by Conqueror's Guidance, which gave them 50 percent more trust and focus. With that, if we attacked from the secret passages, we could capture the forts without taking much damage. Besides, I had my rappas. If I had them work behind the scenes, the situation should tip even more in my favor.

"Unnerstood! If we don't show what we're made of, we ain't even men!" yelled Orcus.

"That's the spirit. I'll go with you, too, so give them everything you have."

"Surely it's too risky for you to—," Leon said, hesitant. As captain of the White Eagles, it was Leon's job to stop me there.

"I know all of you will protect me, so I'm not afraid of anything."

Leon put on his battle face. "The White Eagles will protect you, no matter what!"

Special ability Conqueror's Guidance has leveled up!
Allies' trust and focus will double. Additionally, their offensive and defensive abilities will improve by thirty percent.

Oh, my bonus just got better, too. My troops will be nearly unstoppable now.
"Let's start with the first fort. It was built halfway up the mountain

with the expectation that any attackers would come up the valley path. So we can go around and come in from higher up. We can capture it in no time if our elites go in from above. Let's go!"

The next day came, and at midday we purposely tried taking the valley path, engaging in brief skirmishes with the enemies who came down from the fort. It was all just to make them think we were following the valley.

And then night arrived. We advanced up the ridge path, which was dotted with red ribbons to prevent us from getting lost—something the werewolf rappas had prepped beforehand.

"Jus' leave this to us Red Bears. Twenny people's all we need!"

I decided to leave it to Captain Orcus. Indeed, going into the fort brought risk; it'd be too reckless for me to go. "All right, see it done. There aren't many of them, either. Crush them."

The Red Bears hung down a ladder from the ridge behind the fort and went in one after another. Immediately the air was filled with screams. By the time I descended into the fort, I could hear Orcus saying, "This 'ere's my fifteenth head!" Honestly, my guardsmen had way more training than most troops. Even in small numbers, they showed tremendous ability. By thirty minutes later, almost all our foes were dead, and the fort commander had surrendered.

"Tell us what you know about the other forts if you don't want to die," I threatened the commander. As soon as I had my rappas use their skills at torture, he immediately told us what we wanted. Everything he said was consistent with the information we'd gathered beforehand, so he wasn't lying. The enemy had two forts left. "We can take down the other forts before the day's out. Let's keep going!"

The rappas stole into the next fort and opened the gate from inside. It was the same tactic used on us back when I was sent to Fort Nagraad. A fort is only useful because it's hard to break into. Once a larger enemy force gets in, it turns into a hellish slaughter.

The ridge path from that fort to the next was blocked off, but it didn't matter, since we took a detour. I already had a good grasp of the mountain path there. Here the rappas threw the enemy into disarray by shooting fire.

Now just to overwhelm th——

"Leave this to me, sir," interrupted Meissel Wouge, the former Viscount of Holai, looking especially heroic.

"Fine. Can't get a good piece of them if they just surrender, right? Have at them."

Meissel's troops charged in dauntlessly. The enemy tried desperately to fight back, since if they lost this fort, their plan to stall for time in the valley would fall apart entirely.

I set foot inside the fort myself to inspire the men. "Listen up! If we bring this thing down, we can break through the mountain pass! We can open a giant hole in their defense! Give me this victory!"

I slew three enemy troops myself. Being in the middle of battle activated my special ability Conqueror's Might, which boosted my combat skills twofold.

Sorry, but you can't win with this pathetic lot.

In this clash of wills, our side won out. Around the time I began to think the enemy had been mostly suppressed, Meissel came back. "We killed their commander."

"Well done. Once I take Nagurry, I shall grant you more land."

By the time we'd captured the last fort, it was already fully daytime. We must've actually fought for over twelve hours. Even though I'd been alternating which troops went in, with the travel included, everyone was dog-tired. Nevertheless, taking down three enemy forts in less than a day was a really big deal.

Now that valley path is wide open for us.

After letting the men get their fill of rest, I had them build a camp fortress right at the spot where the mountain pass let out onto the Rentrant Plain, so the enemy could see it. A camp fortress was a temporary staging camp on just a mere earthen embankment. Since we were going to stay for a bit, I did order them to build a sort of shack with an actual roof.

Here, we'd meet up with our troops coming from the rear and then go smash into the enemy's main force. It was as if we held a knife to their throat. They needed to do something to drive us off, but we were ready to go out onto the plain. If word of this plan of ours spread, they'd probably panic, as if a swarm of bees had been let loose in the room.

Finally, Kivik's rearguard unit arrived. "Some of the enemy tried to flank from behind, but we destroyed them. We had more men, though, so it's nothing to boast about." Kivik was quite old, but when it came to war, he was positively bright-eyed and bushy-tailed.

"Well done. Everyone, we have a big fight ahead, but since we're all here, let's come up with a plan." Since I'd broken through the mountain pass, word that Alsrod Nayvil was coming must have begun to spread along the coast, including to Nagurry's capital, Molkara. With Nagurry's situation getting far worse in a short time, the mood there must have been growing increasingly more tense. I'd take advantage of this.

And I had the perfect connection.

I summoned Meissel Wouge. "Under your name, I want you to call for the surrender of any generals you have connections with. If they surrender, I'll guarantee you land. I'll sign all the letters you send, too."

"Understood. There are a number of generals I know from when I was a hostage in Nagurry."

"They're more afraid than I'd thought. It should work. We received another secret letter today." I showed him the letter I'd gotten from the overseer of one of the river-port towns, in which he begged us not to loot. Money and valuables had been sent along with it.

——Ah, this is like our prohibition of temple looting. Asking the enemy to forbid looting can be perceived as siding with them. I'll bet your enemies were already in disarray.

*　　*　　*

If Oda Nobunaga said it, it had to be true.

"This'll all be over if we can get someone in a northern port town to dissent. Know anyone who might fit the bill?"

"Vard Rentrant in the northeast—he may be a Rentrant, but I don't think he's on good terms with the other members of his clan."

"Great, I'll send a messenger right away. Tell him he'll get two extra counties on top of his current territory." It was faster to take action than to think this through. If even one place switched over to our side, it'd give us an advantage.

"There is some risk, however, in delivering a letter by messenger. Will it get there safely...?"

"Don't worry about that. I'll use the rappas."

"Rappas?"

"The ones who work in the shadows of our army."

The plan worked as I thought it would, albeit gradually. Lords with territories far away from the enemy capital at Molkara Castle started surrendering to me little by little. They must've been frightened by the merciless attacks I'd been carrying out. According to spies, Colt Rentrant was having unexpected difficulty gathering troops. One reason might have been that it was the wheat-harvest season, but obviously more and more vassals were afraid because my attack had gone faster than expected.

As an overall principle, I let any generals who didn't fight me directly live. Conversely, ever since I attacked those three counties in my prefecture, it was my practice to kill anyone who pointed a spear at us, with only a few exceptions. They didn't want to cross swords with me directly, thinking of what would happen when they lost.

Some of my men thought I should strike in the meantime, but I instead chose to wait for the enemy to come to me. But that didn't mean I was going to do nothing.

I built small castles along the hills creeping toward the plain. They may have been small, but we ensured they were many. There needed to be enough to meet the enemy's attack.

And finally, Colt Rentrant came before us, leading 4,500 troops—right up to the very middle of the Rentrant Plain, where my forces were now extended. By now I felt confident in my victory. After all, an amazing piece of info had come to us the day before. Vard Rentrant had notified us that he was on our side and would attack Molkara Castle. Thus, in the worst-case scenario, we might be pushed back the first day and have to hold out in a fort in the mountain pass. In the ensuing battle of attrition, with Molkara Castle under attack, Colt would find himself deep in crisis. Now all I had to do was raise my men's morale even higher.

Before the final battle, I rallied my soldiers:

"Listen up. I've led you all this far as Count of Fordoneria. On the other hand, the enemy stands against me as the Count of Nagurry. I'm sure you all know perfectly well which count is worth giving your life for."

I gripped the three-jarg spear in my hand. Perhaps because of my Oda Nobunaga profession, I felt more charismatic than ever before. "The enemy is already as good as defeated—therefore your goal is not to win, but to raze the enemy to the ground! Make the name of Fordoneria resound throughout the world!"

My troops cheered wildly.

I planted the spear into the ground. "Now's the time to show them what you can do with these three-jarg spears!" The second cheer was even greater than the first. I had mustered three thousand men, which honestly was fewer troops than the enemy had. Even so, my men felt as if they couldn't lose. And they wouldn't, as this next battle would soon demonstrate.

The fighting began. Putting their numbers to use, the enemy charged in. Perhaps they'd already heard there was a turncoat in their clan. If so, they needed to defeat me as soon as possible. They couldn't be waiting around to see what move I'd make. On the other hand, our troops maintained their high ground. We'd built little offensive castles all over the place. Our units needed only wait for the enemy to come to them.

And when they did, my men swung their spears.

"What the hell are these spears?!"

"They're too damn long!"

Beaten over the head by our spears, the enemy soldiers fell one after another. The men holding up inside the castles had been training with the three-jarg spears for a long time. We'd completely taken the wind out of the enemy's sails. This was no longer their territory; I'd rebuilt this land for my own purposes.

Of course, I had other tricks up my sleeve. I'd built each forward castle with attack routes that let us easily pick the enemy off with arrows. According to Oda Nobunaga, this was called *yokoya-gakari*. Making the path to the castle entrance twist and turn in a zigzag pattern created more openings in the enemy's defenses, which then allowed our side to reliably shoot them with arrows from multiple locations. Even if they knew it was a trap, they had no choice but to go in, because if they couldn't oust us from here, they'd be in big trouble. Of course, a desperate brute-force attack had no chance of working. It just played even more into our hands.

Unable to capture any of the countless forward castles, the enemy's body count rose and rose. Their general was forced to call a retreat.

Now's the time.

"Red Bears! White Eagles! Battalions under Noen, Kivik, and Meissel—all of you, charge! Skewer each and every one of our foes with your spears!"

""Haaaaah!""

My men shouted like barbarians as we swarmed the opposition. The Tri-Jargs worked wonders in their first real field battle. It was for this day that we'd mass-produced and continuously trained with these spears. With these men, I could even take the kingdom.

The results were instant: We decimated our enemies in the blink of an eye. I could see enemy soldiers fleeing one after another. Neither peasant nor mercenary troops wanted to die. Their leader, Colt Rentrant, narrowly escaped with his life. We killed many of the enemy commanders, so it was a total victory for us.

Even from a propaganda point of view, our victory would have enormous consequences. The Rentrants' subjects who were still unsure would surely forsake their masters.

Not letting up the chase, I continued to pursue Colt Rentrant, and although he had holed up in an old castle, he probably had only about three hundred men. The ones who realized they had no hope of winning must have gotten the hell out.

Ever since the old days, getting destroyed on the battlefield had led to the death of even the greatest powers. Once you took a heavy blow in a large-scale battle, recovery was extremely difficult, and all the more so when it happened in your own territory. Most likely, he'd already heard the report that his capital was being attacked by one of his relatives.

"It's a bit sad for such a prosperous family as the Rentrants to be wiped out so easily, even if it is their destiny," Kivik said thoughtfully, his men surrounding the old castle. "To think these old bones would live to see the end of the Rentrants…"

"I'm going to build my own kingdom while you're alive, you know. Of course, once I conquer another prefecture, I'll have enough work to do that our foreign expeditions will stop for a while. You should rest in the meantime."

"When we've been fighting so long, resting might be the hardest thing of all."

Colt Rentrant, along with the rest of his clan and his top vassals, was too proud to surrender, and most of them committed suicide. I went on with my troops to their capital, Mulkara Castle, but one of the Rentrants there had already surrendered, too, so it was handed over to me by the turncoat Vard Rentrant. With the exception of those who'd previously expressed their intention to surrender, I had many of their clan beheaded. Many of their vassals had switched sides at the very last minute, practically sacrificing their friends, so I killed them for disloyalty. Also, since the women hadn't had a hand in the war, I spared them.

Thus, I took Nagurry Prefecture after securing all of Fordoneria Prefecture in an all-out offensive just two months after unifying Fordoneria.

◇

With my territory growing so drastically, the amount of administrative work I had to do was unlike anything I'd ever seen. Being on the ocean, Nagurry Prefecture had many port towns, and on top of that, I controlled Maust and several downstream river ports on Nagurry River. Simply getting a grasp of these cities took a tremendous amount of time.

"Fanneria, go ahead and find out the size, production, and development potential of these cities and give me a report."

"I'm not sure even someone such as myself could manage this with any haste…" Apparently, it was quite an ordeal even for a financial officer.

"Luckily, most of Nagurry's finance officials have survived. Go ask for their help. I also need to figure out what new land I can give away…" It was a good problem to have, but nevertheless a tough one. Since I had so much more territory, I'd decided to give some away as rewards.

"Captain Orcus Bright of the Red Bears and Captain Leon Milcolaia of the White Eagles: I shall grant you each a county out of Nagurry Prefecture, in recognition of your distinguished service. I shall officially appoint Noen Rowd lord of two of the three counties in north Fordoneria. Meissel Wouge, I'm afraid I can't give you ownership of the county containing Holai Castle, but take Mennal County, the third northern Fordonerian county, as your territory." Those were the bulk of the rewards I gave, although there were others. Meissel was especially happy to be the viscount of a county again.

"Everyone I have mentioned can take the title of viscount. I'll try to see if the royal family will allow it, too."

"My lord, with the royal family in such poor shape, I don't think we even need to ask." Orcus was so upfront about the royal family's situation because he wasn't the sort who cared much about authority. "Even now, the king and his cousin are fighting with each other for control; the royal family ain't even internally unified."

Yes, the conflict between brothers that had begun during the previous generation was still ongoing. The younger brother had become king by ousting his older brother, that older brother's son had taken back the throne, and now the younger brother's son was wandering the land, trying to reclaim the throne for himself. The line of kings was split in two, and neither side seemed to tire of scheming to take down the other.

"Then I'll consult Lord Hasse about making you viscounts."

Most of my vassals present were in shock.

"Who needs permission from a man who could be assassinated at any moment? That there's an empty promise at best," said Orcus.

"Not if Lord Hasse becomes king, right?" I replied, chuckling to myself.

"I plan to force my way into the royal capital to install Lord Hasse as king. And once I do that, I'll...support him as regent, perhaps."

Oda Nobunaga was the first to react.

——Very good! Yes, first you have to control the capital, or you'll get nowhere! I myself first went to the capital with the actual intention of backing the Ashikaga shogun. The thirteenth Ashikaga shogun, Lord Yoshiteru, was quite an extraordinary individual; I met the man myself. After a few years, I wasn't satisfied with supporting the shogun, but still.

Well, setting up a puppet first was standard practice when usurping a country, after all. If it was too early to take over, you could just play it safe as regent.

"I think Lord Hasse's line is better suited for the throne. The current king, Lord Hasse's cousin, only spoils his favorite vassals and flatters the powerful nobles backing him. We need Lord Hasse to be king."

"Supporting a wanderer oughta be a lighter load for us, too." Orcus seemed to catch my meaning. I'd taken two prefectures; now it should be possible to raise nearly ten thousand soldiers. Of course, I had to leave someone at home, so I couldn't take as many troops to the royal capital, but I had enough to make plans with. Going east from Nagurry and then heading inland to the south, I could eventually reach the capital. I had to go through a few prefectures to get there, but it wasn't impossible.

"For now, let's try to find Lord Hasse. I'm sure I heard he's hiding out in a temple in Icht Prefecture, to the southeast of Nagurry. Let's start by tracking him down and giving him protection."

East of Nagurry were Siala Prefecture on the coast and Icht Prefecture farther inland. Icht had an inland culture, and parts of it were split into smaller domains, so it was the perfect place for a wanted man to disappear to.

However, before I could get started on any such political schemes, a big change happened closer to home.

My child had been born.

Men weren't allowed to be present during childbirth. When it came to delivery, women took care of everything. Thus, while praying I'd get good news soon, I went about my work. In a way, it was convenient that I had work to do, as I wouldn't have to get more anxious than necessary. To be honest, I was more worried about the mother's health than the baby's.

Sometime in the evening, Seraphina's lady-in-waiting came running into my office. "The baby is here! It's a boy!"

"Wow, that's great! What about the mother?"

"Yes... Your wife is a bit tired, but no more than normal after a delivery. She's able to hold the baby herself, at least."

"Then everything's perfect!" I stood up from my office desk.

"Ah... Your wife is still quite tired right now, my lord, so might we ask you to wait just a while longer...? Sometimes a newborn's condition can change suddenly, too..."

"Oh... I see... Very well. Please see to the both of them, then." Apparently, the lady-in-waiting was a bit taken aback by my excitement; she was probably worried a man, unused to babies, might drop them. "I do have plenty of work to do, so I'll go visit them later. Tell me when Seraphina's ready."

Before long, I got to see Seraphina again. She was lying in bed with no signs of distress, as the lady-in-waiting had said.

"I did it, darling."

"You did. Now I don't have to worry about an heir." I held her hand.

"We still don't know if he can do it, of course," Seraphina replied, ever the realist.

"I'll make sure he stays healthy. I'm lord of two prefectures—I could get a good doctor from the royal capital."

"I don't only mean his health. You're going to become more and more powerful. We're not yet certain if he will be able to stand under the weight of so much responsibility. I mean, Laviala's child might be smarter, for one." Seraphina was eerily levelheaded about all this.

"I always thought a mother would want her own to be heir."

"I want to be the wife of a hero first and foremost. I wouldn't want to compromise our country by picking the wrong heir."

"I'm glad to have such a wise wife as you." I took the baby into my arms. "It's hard to tell if it's a boy or a girl, isn't it?"

"It always is!" she laughed.

The baby looked at me but didn't seem to know what was going on. That was only natural, I suppose. I thought he would start crying, but he just had a constant vacant look. "One day, I'll have much land you won't even know where the name Nayvil comes from. That could be fifteen or twenty years from now, who knows, but it'll all be yours someday."

That's your job and your destiny.

"Darling, he doesn't understand anything you say."

Of course. I know that much. I just had the urge to tell him all of a sudden.

——All men act soft around their children. Including me. They will never be cuter than they are at this age, though, especially since they don't give lip.

Oda Nobunaga, you think he's cute, too?

——Another person's baby might as well be a monkey. However… if this little one proves helpful in your work as a conqueror, I suppose he might entertain me in the long run.

I'll…choose to believe he's congratulating me.

My entire domain was full of celebration following the birth. Lots of people came excitedly to pay respects, which was a lot to deal with as always. Of course, there was one other thing left on my mind.

Two months after Seraphina gave birth, Laviala's baby was about to be born. I'd heard that babies of half-elves stayed in the womb for a longer time than those of regular humans, so there was nothing unusual about it schedule-wise, but…

"It seems the baby is coming feetfirst, so the mother is having some trouble…," one of the ladies-in-waiting informed me. It made me a nervous wreck.

"How is Laviala?"

"My lord, I assure you I will make certain Lady Laviala is safe…"

I went to a temple in Maust outside the castle—completely out of character for me—and prayed that everything would be all right. At times like these, all a man could do was pray.

——So you have a pious side, too.

Quiet, you. I don't need my profession's input.

——I, too, wanted to look to the gods for help on several occasions. But ultimately, the gods are just a crutch. In the end, people have to forge their own destiny. But when it comes to a mother and her baby's health, there is little that can be done aside from praying. Pray with all your might; I shall join you.

Who would have thought I'd receive emotional support from my job?

I wondered how the priest might react if I told him about this. Next to me was Elnarta, the priest who'd bestowed me with the Oda Nobunaga profession. I'd summoned him to Maust around the time I took it. In his mind, it was probably the gods, not him, who'd bestowed my profession, but I wanted him with me just in case.

As I was praying at the statue of a deity, someone came and stood alongside me. Standing next to the count seemed highly disrespectful to me, but I soon realized who this person was.

"Seraphina, I hadn't heard you'd be here…"

"Yes, because I didn't tell you. But the gods bestowed me with the job of Saint—doesn't it make sense for me to be here?"

She then knelt down and began to pray earnestly, sending phrases woven of ancient words to the gods. It demonstrated her specialized education and cultured upbringing. I was once again struck by how angelic she was. Seraphina was a prideful person, but she had always put in the appropriate effort.

At last, Seraphina's prayer came to an end. She finally bowed her head to the statue.

"Darling, I want to be your guardian angel—no, a goddess."

"I truly am glad you're my wife. If we weren't in the temple, I'd want to hold you tight right now."

The Saint's prayer seemed to have been heard. Upon my return to Maust Castle, a lady-in-waiting brought word of Laviala's delivery. "You have a baby girl!"

"How is Laviala?" For me, having lost both of my parents at a young age, Laviala was just as much family as Altia.

The lady-in-waiting smiled and replied, "Yes, Lady Laviala managed quite well!"

I was deeply relieved. "I think I was more anxious about this than any battle."

I announced a domain-wide tax reduction for the next year. I wanted to win over the hearts of the Nagurrians anyway, so it might've been perfect timing. When I saw Laviala afterward, we hugged each other, crying.

"Thank you for having my child."

"I'm so happy I could do this for you…"

Not long after I'd become the father of two children, I turned twenty-one years old. It was probably the most eventful year of my life, for someone like me to go from controlling zero prefectures to two. No one would've believed it a year ago if you'd told them. What's more, right after I turned twenty-one, once again something momentous happened politically. We discovered the location of the royal family's Lord Hasse, who then came to us at Maust Castle.

◇

Hasse looked rather uncomfortable when he appeared before me. Though he was just a bit older than I, at twenty-five years old, he looked much more haggard.

The reason was simple. Hasse had no titles.

Really, as the current king's cousin and the son of the previous king—and considering kingdom precedents—he could've easily had the title of duke or a position as viceroy. However, the current king, Paffus VI, treated Hasse as a criminal and had stripped him of his titles. As far as Hasse was concerned, Paffus VI wanted to secure the throne for his own line by ending his cousin's. Of course, Hasse was not a pushover who would allow himself to be killed after being painted as a criminal, but living as a nomad probably had made him somewhat subservient. It was twelve years ago that Hasse's father, the previous king, Grandora III, was forced to leave the capital during an attack by his nephew Paffus. So for a full twelve years, Hasse had no choice but to live as a wanderer. Grandora III died of illness three years after being driven from the capital.

"Lord Fordoneria, I came here upon hearing you would offer me your support... Is that really true?"

"Actually, I would like to hear your reason for doubting my intentions. Why should I try to fool *his majesty the crown prince*?"

I deliberately used the term *crown prince*.

"Crown prince? Me?" Hasse pointed to himself with a bewildered expression.

"Yes, you. Please ask yourself this: Has the Kingdom of Therwil ever

© Kaito Shibano

been at peace during the more than ten years since the current king's reign began? There's nothing but war everywhere. It's a miracle the capital hasn't been burned to the ground."

The country was a mess, and that was a fact. I could point out any number of failings. Of course, things were already disastrous by the time Paffus VI took the throne, so while he probably wouldn't accept blame for everything, as the monarch, he couldn't avoid being criticized for it.

I continued, "Even in the capital, the struggle for power has led to continuous replacement of the chancellor, assassination of government ministers, and more. This proves that everyone serving the king is only thinking of their own gain, not of the people. If you make a hut using rotten supports, it will fall apart. It has to be remade. And so..." I looked Hasse firmly in the eye. "There is no one who should be king but you. In order to rebuild the Kingdom of Therwil, I ask that you please take the throne. I, Alsrod Nayvil, am prepared to lay down my life to see it done."

I could see a fire light in Hasse's eyes. No doubt this man had also dreamed of becoming king, lighting that fire was certainly not difficult. No matter how unstable the throne was, almost anyone would want to be king.

"Very well. I, too, have found the current king's behavior to be most insufferable. I shall become king and restore the Kingdom of Therwil to its former glory!"

"That's the spirit. Now, let's go ahead and spread word both here and abroad that you are the crown prince."

"What do you mean, my lord?"

"If many lords of other realms come to pay homage to you, everyone should see your majesty for what it is."

"I see!" Hasse's eyes burned ever brighter. He must have spent the majority of his days not knowing what tomorrow would bring. If he could have a ceremony unifying the nobility under him, it was no wonder he'd be pleased.

"First, let us write to lords everywhere, requesting they come pay respects at Maust Castle. I will also send my own letter to them."

Needless to say, if the lords of other lands gathered at Maust Castle, they would see my majesty, as well. If we captured the royal capital, everyone would expect me to take the position of regent at least. Of course, I expected some trouble for the ceremony.

Seraphina, for one, looked uncertain. "Darling, I understand what you want here—really, I do. But try putting yourself in my father's shoes." Her father—my father-in-law—Ayles Caltis, the Count of Brantaar, was expanding his territory by continuing to attack northward, while being allied to me. "If he comes to Maust Castle to pay respects to Lord Hasse, people might see that as him bowing before you. I mean, your territory is bigger now than his, but still…"

"True. I suppose it's not enough to leave it to you, is it?" Of course, whether such a highly influential man in this region as Ayles came would completely change anyone's impression of me. I wanted him to come at all costs.

"You'll need an excellent gift. Otherwise, I think he'll say he's ill and decide not to come."

"Fine. I'll get him a present, then," I replied plainly. And so I promptly sent my father-in-law a letter.

As it turned out, Ayles accepted my terms.

◇

Five months after Hasse came to Maust Castle, we held his ceremony, with the rulers of other lands assembled.

"I shall be the next king. This cannot be denied."

Several rulers came to Maust Castle that day: the lord of Olbia Prefecture, home of my sister's husband, Brando Naaham; the lord of Icht Prefecture, where Hasse had been in hiding; Ayles Caltis, ruler of Brantaar Prefecture, also known as Mineria; and others. They certainly weren't lords from all over the kingdom. Still, Ayles and I controlled over three prefectures between the two of us, and if you considered the prefectures represented by the lords who came, the number was almost ten. In particular, many small lords, like the ones neighboring Icht Prefecture or Ayles's territory, came to the ceremony out of fear of retribution should they not attend. This way, it was easy to tell who in neighboring domains would obey and who would oppose me. I was undeniably powerful enough that I couldn't be ignored as a threat to the current king.

And then, my gift was presented to Ayles. "Ayles Caltis, to reward your unwavering loyalty up until now, as the crown prince, I grant you the title of marquess. Nobility titles shall also be given to each member of your clan. I am additionally appointing you as the pacification governor-general of West Therwil. Let all rebels be slain!"

Ayles said, "I am most grateful for this gift" and accepted the title. Yes, I'd made him a higher rank than myself. I'd just given him even greater justification to carry out his wars of invasion. Naturally, the kingdom wouldn't recognize such a thing, but since the king was too weak to come attack this far away anyway, it didn't make a difference. Leading the crown prince east, I'd take the fight to the king.

♡

Because Ayles Caltis had come to Maust Castle, I took the opportunity to hold a meeting. When he was holding his grandchild, his face was that of a jolly old man, but when he was alone with me, I could see the ruthless man I knew he was, even when he wasn't saying or doing anything.

"I never expected you to take out the Rentrants so soon. Your talent is truly frightening."

"Judging by the terrain, I decided going straight through the mountain pass would turn things in my favor. Capturing the forts was somewhat of a gamble, but since they weren't expecting it, I figured it was a good bet."

"Yes, and that's what's so frightening about you." A bitter smile crossed Ayles's face. He'd turned somewhat grayer than the last time we'd met. "I consider myself a decisive man. I've even prevented rebellion before by purging anyone I found suspicious, even my top vassals.

I've got plenty of confidence there. But you're frighteningly good at war itself…" The primary emotion behind his bitter smile seemed to be real fear. "Just like when you defended Fort Nagraad. You show a genius ability for battle itself. Otherwise, your designs on Nagurry would've taken at least five years. You used war as a weapon to make quick work of them in the blink of an eye…"

"I take action, believing the gods are on my side. After all"—I took a sip of the alcohol on the table—"a hero capable of building a country ought to have divine protection from the start. If they weren't so blessed, everything would end halfway through."

"Building a country, huh…? That may not be as ludicrous as it sounds…" Ayles let out a sigh. "I just ask you not to take my sons' and daughters' lands. I love my other children besides Seraphina, too."

"Go ahead and keep expanding for yourself, sir—I won't interfere. I wouldn't treat my wife's father so coldly. You have my word."

"Very well," Ayles replied.

Thus, in reality, I came to be above Ayles.

◇

Hasse's claim that he was the crown prince seemed to have caused quite a stir in the royal capital. The royal dynasty announced its decision to strip the titles and territory of all the lords who had come to visit Hasse, though obviously it didn't have the power to enforce it. No lord around me could challenge me head-to-head, so it wasn't even a threat. The currently ruling Paffus VI had been stripped of his rank when he rebelled against Grandora III in the first place. In other words, even the king's orders had only a relative value by this point.

"…With the royal line split in two, even the king's orders are rather meaningless, aren't they?" remarked my concubine Fleur. She was reading the letter that had come ordering I hand over the crown prince. I was lying on her lap. After the big job of instating Hasse and assembling the other lords, I'd wanted a breather.

"They certainly are. The lords who are on the king's bad side can turn things around by supporting the opposition. That sort of thing has happened over and over throughout the Hundred Years' Rebellion, so the king's authority has fallen even lower. As they say, you reap what you sow."

"The temples are in a frenzy, too. Especially the temples that have always been guaranteed control of their estate by praying for the royal family's stability—apparently they're not sure whether to side with you or not."

"You've really helped me get the temples' land sorted out. Thanks, Fleur." Her negotiation skills were truly remarkable; she'd met with many temple priests and summarized the situation for me in detail. I now knew quite well which temples were my allies and which were my enemies. Thus, I also knew which I needed to protect and which I didn't.

"I am glad to be of service."

I got out of my seat and held Fleur close. "Enough with the formalities. You're one of my wives, too. Call me dear, at least."

"Thank you very much, d-dear..."

Seraphina and Laviala were still tired from giving birth. I visited them both regardless, but I was invariably spending more and more time in Fleur's room now. It wasn't all about indulgence, though. Fleur had a very shrewd sense for politics, which proved extremely helpful. I needed to make concrete plans for invading the capital next.

"Come to think of it, one of Lord Hasse's vassals is quite a capable individual, one who had long worked very hard to ensure Lord Hasse and his family could live comfortably. I also heard this vassal is a dwarf."

"A dwarf? He has a dwarf?"

Fleur had a different way of looking at people than I did. When I thought of dwarves, I could think only of bearded warriors, even if they weren't all like that. Among them were even famous garden designers specializing in landscape architecture.

"Oh, and she's a dwarf woman. Apparently, she's not a court lady but rather a female knight who entered his service. I believe her name is something like Kelara Hilara."

"Dwarves have the weirdest names. But I got it. I'll see if I can meet her."

To be honest, though, I was doubtful. I didn't think there was anyone so capable among Hasse's vassals. If they were skilled, surely they could've found someone else to serve. Maybe he just preferred this knight? However, when I summoned her to me, she was not at all what I'd expected.

"I have arrived, my lord. My name is Kelara Hilara, guardian knight of Lord Hasse. I come from a line of tax collectors from a poor village in the west. Four generations ago, we came as soldiers to the capital, where I was raised together with Lord Hasse."

I'd had the impression that many dwarf women were small, but her height wasn't much different from mine. Her skin was the distinctive dark brown of dwarves, and her voice and mannerisms were just as refined as those of a young noble of good birth.

"I heard you took care of ceremonies, following the old ways befitting the royal family, even while Lord Hasse lived as a wanderer," I replied. "May I ask you about those old customs?"

"Understood. Well, first is the ceremony of the new year..." Kelara began to describe all the yearly ceremonies without skipping a beat. What was shocking was that not only had she memorized the order of the ceremonies, but she even talked about what to omit and what to replace it with, based on her knowledge of where the ceremonies came from and past precedents. "...And so it's proper etiquette to bestow a sword upon the vassal, but as its history only traces back to about a hundred years ago, I made it more old-fashioned by omitting that element. Next is—"

"No, that's enough. I get it."

Damn, she's brilliant! Kelara, huh... I'd like to hire her. I've never had anyone like her in my servitude before.

"Dame Kelara Hilara, if possible, will you not serve me as well? Until a few years ago, I was just a small rural lord, you see. I don't know much about ancient customs, so I don't even know what I need to follow as a count. If I bring shame on myself, so be it, but if I'm not careful, I might bring shame on the crown prince."

It was good to be at least half-genuine about these sorts of things. I was nearing a position where I could no longer ignore good manners. It certainly wasn't a plus to be thought of as a country bumpkin who was only good at war. When I got to the capital, I wouldn't be able to gain the confidence of the aristocracy. Historically, barbarian-like warlords had taken the capital several times before, but because they hadn't respected the rituals, they'd been hated by the aristocracy and nearby lords, eventually leading to their own downfall.

"If you'll have me, my lord." Even the smallest of her mannerisms gave me the impression of a royal guard. She also smelled faintly of incense—very fitting for a female warrior.

——I do not trust her, although I cannot say exactly why.

Oda Nobunaga looked scornful, though—not that I could see his face, of course.

——She reeks of Mitsuhide. He was also well-educated and clever, but he turned on me. Of course, Mitsuhide was already much older than this young lady at the time.

Oh, so she reminds you of someone who betrayed you.

——Not only did he betray me, he killed me at Honnouji.

Ho-no-ji? Is that a place or something? I mean, this Oda Nobunaga fellow seems like the type to do whatever he pleases, so it's no surprise he had some traitors among his ranks.

——Be careful. Anyone who's mastered the old ways is a conservative. And conservatives will eventually clash with a revolutionary like you.

That's more or less a given, so I'll have to be careful. Someone who never misses a prayer at the temple certainly isn't going to be saying the royal dynasty and everything with it needs to be destroyed and remade.

"Now then, Kelara, I'll grant you land, as well. I won't force you to serve only me or make any other equally ridiculous demands, so don't worry."

"Thank you very much." Kelara thanked me politely, but she wasn't smiling. For one person to have multiple masters was not impossible, so there shouldn't be a problem. It certainly would be bad if she was the crown prince's lover, though. I might as well check to be sure. It would be foolish to incur his ill will for that.

"By the way, the crown prince won't be jealous of your service to me, will he? If the two of you have any sort of intimate relationship, I'll keep my distance."

"You needn't worry about such trifles. The crown prince isn't interested in dwarves. Ever since the first king, it's been said that members of the royal family are forbidden from having children with elves or dwarves."

"I see. I apologize for the absurd question."

For now, I was glad to be free of that worry. Afterward, in my spare time, I learned about various etiquettes and academics from Kelara. I was sure I'd had at least a minimal education, but only one befitting of a rural lord. Kelara had apparently had the best education in the capital hammered into her from an early age, and even in exile, she was around scholars. By now she must've had enough knowledge to make a name as a scholar herself. Of course, this was all in my spare time. My attack plans were also making steady progress.

I first extended my reach to Icht Prefecture, located inland to the east. Icht had no powerful lords, and some of the small lords had come to pay respects to Hasse, meaning I could make use of Hasse's authority. The problem was the lords who hadn't come to submit to Hasse—I'd have to take them down one by one. On the other hand, also to the east, but on the coast, was Siala Prefecture, about two-thirds of which was controlled by the Antoini clan.

Siala had one powerful count, but not one powerful enough to pose any threat to me. Besides, there were other powerful and mostly independent viscounts in the prefecture. All I had to do was disrupt their unity, and things would simply fall into place.

I carried out the invasion of Icht Prefecture somewhat cautiously. The reason was that I needed time to firmly remake Nagurry as my own territory. If my territory expanded too quickly, the mechanisms of control would remain in a state of chaos. Thinking of the future, I steadily strengthened my control over the port towns. By putting them all under my direct rule, I concentrated wealth for myself. With that wealth, I expanded the numbers of my guardsmen to make them into the strongest troops around. During the year or so after Hasse formally became crown prince, I placed nearly all of Icht Prefecture under my control. At twenty-two years old, I became lord of three prefectures. I was another step closer to taking control of the capital.

I spoke alone with Laviala about where to send troops going forward. Not only that—

"I think it's about time I made my return to the battlefield!"

—but Laviala had her own fervent wishes. Indeed, she'd spent all of the past year fulfilling her role as both mother to our daughter and wet nurse to Seraphina's son. Laviala herself knew better than anyone that these were her top priorities, and so she had faithfully performed her duties as needed.

At the end of the day, however, her real profession was Archer. Apparently, she had never ceased to think of herself as a combatant.

"I never once neglected to practice my archery whenever I had the time. I'm sure I can be of help the moment a war breaks out!"

"It's not your skills I'm concerned about. It's just, when it comes to war, you'd have to be away from the children…" There was no way to justify bringing children a year and a few months old onto the battlefield.

"Well... I'd have to have someone else look after them, just for that time..."

"I can't say I'm happy to take my own wife to the battlefield, but that's your nature as a warrior..." I didn't have any right to stop her when I'd always willfully put myself in harm's way. Regardless, I wasn't the type to just roll over for nothing.

Just then, I had an idea. "All right, come with me in the next war. It'll be in Olbia. The enemy isn't even that strong."

"Oh? I thought you were going to carve a path to the capital."

"I'm sure I'll attack Siala eventually, but first I'm going to put Brando Naaham in my debt. I hear a group of lords is trying to ally against him." Once I'd secured my southern flank, I'd attack east. "Also, I'd like to try using the dwarf woman Kelara as a commander."

There was no good time to test people with unknown skills when all your wars were critically important, so uninspiring wars like this were valuable, too. Brando Naaham would be happy, too; as an extreme example, arriving with three or four thousand soldiers would be quite intimidating to the enemy.

"Ah, that scholar knight?" Laviala's gaze turned icy. "Do you perhaps mean to take her as a wife? A woman like that doesn't make a good consort, you know."

"Hey, hey, I'm no lecher... Besides, I can't be going only to your room all the time, either."

I was making sure to visit Seraphina's, Fleur's, and also Laviala's chambers so they wouldn't feel as if I was neglecting any of them. Of course, all three of them were beautiful, so it wasn't as if I hated our visits. I knew of past kings who'd run themselves ragged or shirked their duties because they'd spent too much time with their consorts. I was being careful not to let anything like that happen.

"S-sorry... I understand your position, too. Lady Seraphina and I chose Miss Fleur because we thought she would be good for you... But you must get lonely with so few women around..."

"Don't worry—there's nothing going on between Kelara and me. I'm only using her because she's capable."

"By the way, I heard Lady Altia was blessed with a child, too. A girl, apparently."

Now it was my turn to look annoyed. "I swear, if I'd been born a king, I would've put her in a convent for sure…"

"You're every bit as selfish as I am, Lord Alsrod."

"Excuse me? I think you need to be punished." I suddenly reached around her side.

"Lord Alsrod, I told you I'm sensitive there… Ah, that tickles! I said no! Ah-ha-ha! Ha-ha-ha!"

Oh, I know it does. We've been together long enough by now.

Leading 3,500 troops, I advanced south. I wasn't joining up with Brando Naaham, but instead I was going to attack the confederation of lords in northwest Olbia to keep him from getting pincered. The area was mountainous, just like the rest of Olbia; guerrilla tactics in a place like this would be hell to fight off.

"Kelara, I'm giving you three hundred men. Give it your best."

"Understood."

Let's see what you can do.

Royal guards typically didn't have experience commanding a large number of troops. However, as long as she was in my camp, she might have to lead a few thousand in some cases. I wanted to see whether she could handle it. Laviala, on the other hand, went into the countryside once I gave her permission. Perhaps because of her elf blood, apparently she actually got more motivated when the fighting took place within a forest. The enemy wasn't that strong anyway, so I figured it'd be all right.

After a while, Kelara returned, looking unfazed. She was so calm, it was almost as if we weren't on a battlefield. Her expression was just as if she were reading a book. It wasn't a commanding look, either; she had more of the air of a civil servant than of a general. Of course, an uncivilized mountain-man type wouldn't really be fit to lead a large army anyway.

"You came back awfully soon. Did it not go well?"

"We slaughtered three enemy generals."

"Wow! That's great for such a short time!"

Results, indeed.

With the fight taking place in a mountainous area, it was practically impossible to destroy the enemy completely. Keeping that in mind, it was fair to say she did very well.

"Is your profession something helpful in battle perchance?" I asked.

If you think about it, since she was a female knight, it wouldn't be unexpected for her to have a job like Fencer or General.

"No, I don't have any such special talents. All I did was use what I thought to be the best tactics per the writings of military strategy both past and present." Calm and collected as always.

"In a way, that fighting style is perfect for you. Can you keep it up?"

"Yes. I will do whatever my lord commands."

Eventually, Kelara went on to kill over five more enemy commanders. She had more success than Laviala, who'd only recently returned to the battlefront. Of course, Laviala was more of a lone wolf, so it was like comparing apples to oranges.

We'd dealt a huge blow to the enemy lords, and with almost no harm to our side. Brando would certainly be thankful. The operation was a huge success.

I'd gotten to see what Kelara could do, in particular. It wasn't anything flashy, but her ability to reliably defeat the enemy was worth admiring. If she was this good, she wouldn't make any big mistakes if I gave her a large army.

"You did better than anyone else in this war," I said to Kelara as we rode back from our victory to Maust Castle.

"It is an honor to hear you say so, my lord."

Speaking of, I'd forgotten to ask her something before: "Kelara, just what *is* your profession?"

"Actually…it's a highly peculiar job, so many people don't believe me…" Kelara looked just a bit gloomy.

So even a woman like her gets uncomfortable at times. "I won't question it. Tell me."

"Yes, sir. I'm not quite sure of its meaning, but my job is 'Akechi Mitsuhide'…"

My heart skipped a beat. I was sure I'd heard that name somewhere…

——This old conqueror was right on the money.

Hey, don't congratulate yourself just yet.

——Alsrod, be careful. This woman may betray you. Her job is Akechi Mitsuhide, after all.

I, however, actually thought this made things interesting. This "Akechi Mitsuhide" or whatever would be mine to command. He was one of Oda Nobunaga's top vassals anyway, right? That was proof he would be incredibly useful.

"Kelara, can you hear this…Akechi's voice?"

"No—can professions even speak? And yet, with this job of mine, I find it easier to remember things about old palace customs. It's like I can naturally recall what was written where…"

"Yeah, you're right! Hearing voices would be totally ridiculous, wouldn't it?"

It seemed her job was fundamentally different from my Oda Nobunaga one. Maybe it was just related to the skills of this Akechi Mitsuhide to whom it referred?

——I suppose only a man of my caliber can be self-aware as a profession.

A job that could talk was certainly more amusing. I mean, two heads are better than one, and more than anything, it was a great way to pass the time.

Let's get to the capital soon, Oda Nobunaga.

——Of course. The throne is yours to take.

END

I had the ceremony for my twentieth birthday at my home, Nayvil Castle. In the Kingdom of Therwil, it was customary to have a simple ceremony for men and women who had just turned twenty. Of course, it was really no more than a short formality ending within thirty minutes at most, but it was a sort of rite of passage. In this country, there was no strictly set age at which you became an adult, so different rites of passage coexisted, including both the profession-bestowal ceremony and this twentieth-birthday ceremony. Or if I'd been the oldest legitimate child and my father had still been alive, succession also would have occurred around this time.

"I think I'll probably eventually move my capital to Maust, but it's nice enough to celebrate my twentieth birthday in my hometown," I said in front of my vassals in attendance. Of course, I didn't exactly have *all* my vassals assembled together. I'd ordered that they prioritize any other work they had. This was not a period of peace and tranquility. Ceremonies meant nothing if you lost your territory in the meantime.

A priest came over and poured some alcohol into my glass. When I drank this, it would mean the ceremony had come to a close.

——This is like our coming-of-age ceremony. We called it *genpuku*.

So your world had something similar, too.

——But unlike my world, you people don't change your names. Actually, the Japanese might have changed their names too much.

Like the one I remember as Kenshin—I can't even remember how many times he changed his.

Good thing we didn't have that system. It might be fine for yourself, but remembering your vassals' names would be so troublesome if they were changing all the time.

I imbibed the somewhat mediocre drink, a few vassals gave their congratulations, and the ritual ended. As my vassals slowly filed out of the ceremony room, Laviala remained, motionless.

"What is it, Laviala? Was something different from your twentieth birthday?" Laviala had already had her ceremony, since she was less than a year older than I was. There weren't as many attendees at hers as there were at mine, since I was a count now, but otherwise everything was mostly the same.

"Lord Alsrod, I would like some of your time after noon tomorrow; is that acceptable?"

"Noon? Well, I don't have any work I can't delegate, so it's not impossible."

"Yes, I know you don't," Laviala answered, smiling sweetly. She already had a good idea of my work schedule, of course. In other words, I had no right to refuse. "Well, please come to my chambers then. Thank you!" she said cheerfully and left the ceremony room. But just what did she want, telling me to come to her chambers after noon...? If it was about something classified, she wouldn't have said it so happily, either. Maybe it really was something for...you know...behind closed doors? Couldn't that just wait for nighttime? I couldn't just ask if that was it, either...

"Brother." Aside from me, Altia was the only one still left in the room. She was almost never around during my official duties, but since this was a ceremony for close relations, she'd been in attendance, too. She looked at me a bit disdainfully. "Brother, you were thinking something indecent when Miss Laviala invited you to her room just now, weren't you?"

I was embarrassed to be asked so directly. Altia seemed to have good ears for these sorts of things as of late. The reason was clear: Seraphina had been putting ideas in her head.

"As the sister of a count, you really ought to think before you speak."

"Oh, I know. That's why I'm speaking when no one's around."

"Either way, this is none of your concern. In fact, thinking nothing of what she said would itself be strange. My thoughts were totally normal."

Her expression still didn't change—although that was hardly unusual, as she wasn't really the type to smile cheerfully.

"Hmm, I wonder if Miss Laviala would be pleased to know that. Well, see you."

Altia left the room with a lady-in-waiting in tow. I then realized she hadn't said a word about my birthday, not even during the ceremony. As her older brother, that made me just a bit sad. I'd been so careful to raise her as a respectable young lady, too…

The next day, just as I'd promised Laviala, I finished my work by morning's end and went to her chambers. I told my other vassals I had an important job to attend to. I was known as a hardworking ruler who almost never took breaks, after all, so I had to have a reason. Though I wasn't pretending to be a hardworking ruler; I naturally had much more work to do with all my new territory. I knocked on Laviala's door.

"Come in," said Laviala's voice from inside.

I am a count, you know…, I thought, but getting angry at Laviala—who'd always treated me as a little brother—wouldn't do any good, so I opened the door. Just as I did, I felt the presence of several others. I reflexively started to back out, thinking there might be an assassin lying in wait. It was hard to think of a good reason why several people would be in Laviala's room. Did I make a mistake? I should've been more cautious. A ruler had countless people who wanted to kill him. If I was murdered here, I'd amount to only one of a zillion other wannabe warlords in this chaotic age…

"Happy birthday, Lord Alsrod!"

"Happy birthday, darling!"

"Happy birthday, brother."

Three voices spoke one after another. In front of me stood Laviala, and to the left and right stood Seraphina and Altia, respectively. And all three of them were holding bright-pink flowers.

"Ah, so that's what this is all about…" Once I realized what was going on, I instantly relaxed. They really should've congratulated me for not passing out right there.

"Here, Lord Alsrod, these flowers are for you!" Laviala handed me the most magnificent bouquet of the three. If I refused to accept after all this, I couldn't complain if they started an insurrection. I took it firmly in both hands.

"I'll happily accept them, Laviala."

She pulled the arm I'd cradled the flowers in. "All right, don't just stand there; please come over to the table. We've got some delicious tea and dessert for you!" Now I was nothing more than little brother being dragged along by his big sister, and I sat down. The whole room was adorned with colorful paper decorations, apparently just for this day.

Looking at my consort, I asked, "This was all your idea, wasn't it, Seraphina?"

She made a show of puffing out her cheeks. "Well, excuse me! Laviala was the one who brought this up. She said you've never had anyone celebrate your birthday before."

"Well, I lost my mother when I was little. My father was busy with work, and nobody cared about me. My family wasn't important enough."

Back then, nobody had expected I'd ever have authority. And neither had I, honestly. So who would even want to celebrate me?

"So I told Miss Laviala we should have a nice little party. I mean, twenty years old is the perfect occasion, too.'"

"So you *were* a part of this, huh?"

"Oh hush! I only gave her a little inspiration. I'm like the pitch for a torch. Pitch doesn't just burn on its own," she said, sounding even more mischievous than usual.

"Lord Alsrod, surely you can at least take one day off a year to relax like this, yes? I'll get you some tea." Laviala poured tea from the pot into a teacup. A faintly bitter aroma filled my nose.

"True. It might be good to have a day like this sometimes. Thanks, Laviala. I mean, thank you, everyone." I turned to Altia, who'd taken a seat. "So this was why you were acting so cold yesterday." Just moments

© Kaito Shibano

ago she'd wished me a happy birthday. As her older brother, that made me truly happy. Altia was the only blood relative I had.

"I was disappointed in you, thinking dirty things when Miss Laviala asked you to come to her," she replied icily.

"Oh, can't you let it go?! It was an honest mistake!"

"Oh my, why don't you give Miss Laviala a kiss, darling?" Seraphina was instigating again. *Well, if I were alone with Laviala here, I would've long since given her a kiss on my own.* But my wife and my sister were here; it was more natural to have self-control.

"But won't it bother you? I mean, you're my wife."

"Come now, I'm not nearly that stuffy. It's just a kiss, so go ahead, as you please."

I couldn't not do it after being told that. "Kiss her," Altia urged me on. She wanted Laviala and me to be happy together.

I got up slowly and stood in front of Laviala. "Laviala, may I kiss you?"

"Yes, Lord Alsrod."

We'd already looked into each other's eyes more times than I could count, but the gaze we shared then seemed like something very special. I wrapped my arm around her back, drew her close, and pressed my lips to hers. I'd been with Laviala for only twenty years. If possible, I wanted to still be living with her for ten or even twenty more. Really, I wanted to keep kissing her longer, but—

Seraphina and Altia were clapping their hands to make a point. "Darling, isn't that a little long? Any more and I might have to go back home to my father."

Right. Can't neglect my wife too much. Even with a smile on her face, she might have been plotting something devious. "Yes, I should make things fair." Not even waiting for a reply, I gave Seraphina a swift kiss where she sat.

"Oh, darling, you're so mean…" She was flustered but didn't altogether seem to mind—which was why I'd done it.

"Brother, when did you turn into a philanderer?" Sure enough, my sister was glaring at me again, but that was neither here nor there.

"As they say, great men are great lovers. It's proof I'm becoming a great man."

Afterword

Nice to meet you—or perhaps nice to see you again. Thank you so much for picking up *A Mysterious Job Called Oda Nobunaga*! This work was originally (or rather, still is) a serialized novel on the website Shousetsuka ni Narou.

At the time, the site's rankings had many stories involving an unusual profession in a parallel world. (At least, that's my personal impression, not backed by data...) That made me wonder whether I could maybe take a stab at a war story, something I'd always wanted to try, by adding some kind of unusual profession to it.

Right around the same time, my historical novel (purely a historical novel) *Date Elf Masamune*, which I was writing for GA Bunko, was reaching its climax. It was full of enemies, like Oda Nobunaga as Satan, Toyotomi Hideyoshi as Hanuman, and Tokugawa Ieyasu as the Yeti. So I naturally had the idea to try putting Sengoku-period references into a fantasy war story.

Of course, at first I couldn't come up with a good idea for a profession; my thought process went like this: "*Ashigaru*? Too plain. Warrior's probably been done to death by now... I could say they're an unmatched gunman, but those came from Europe, the home of fantasy..." As I racked my brain over what profession to choose, I had a brilliant (?) idea: I'll make a job called Oda Nobunaga!

Thus was born this work, where the protagonist is a young lord with the profession Oda Nobunaga. With everyone's help, it earned first place in both the daily and weekly rankings on Shousetsuka ni Narou.

Thank you so much to all those who gave their support back when it was a web novel. For those of you starting with the book, I'm still posting new parts online, so please take a look there, too!

Next, I have to give credit to the illustrator, Kaito Shibano: Thank you so, so much for your beautiful artwork! You can feel the spirit and bravery of the protagonist, Alsrod; he looks super-cool! That's why—and I think this might be a first for any of my books—I decided to have only a male character on the cover!

Of course, the leading ladies, like the half-elf Laviala, are gorgeous enough to drool over, too. I'm jealous of Alsrod, and I'm the author. Ha-ha.

Thank you so much, too, to everyone who purchased this book! GA Bunko also published the third volume of *I've Been Killing Slimes for 300 Years...* on the same day, and that series is getting a manga adaptation by Yusuke Shiba for Gangan GA. It's another really fun story, so I'd be thrilled if you checked it out as well!

Respectfully yours,

Kisetsu Morita